BS

The Big House

The Big House

HELENA McEWEN

BLOOMSBURY

FGG090   £12·99

First published 2000
Copyright © 2000 by Helena McEwen

The moral right of the author has been asserted
Bloomsbury Publishing Plc, 38 Soho Square, London W1V 5DF

A CIP catalogue record for this book
is available from the British Library

ISBN 0 7475 4637 1

10 9 8 7 6 5 4 3 2

Typeset by Hewer Text Ltd, Edinburgh
Printed in Great Britain by Clays Ltd, St Ives plc

For J and K.

'You go, it's your turn.'

'No, it's yours!'

'It is not!'

'It's hers, isn't it, Specky?' James turns to me.

'Don't get me involved in this,' I laugh.

They're sitting round the square table in the old nursery, painting with watercolours and one glass of muddy water.

'I changed it last time!'

'You're a liar! I changed it five minutes ago,' says Kitty in a squeaky voice. I can't help laughing, in their twenties, still squabbling like kids.

It means walking a few steps through to the pantry and pouring the water down the sink.

'Anyway, you're the one using all that dark blue.'

'Look, I'll change it,' I say, getting off the sofa and picking up the glass. The water is grey-brown, the colour it always goes.

'Yes!' says James as though I've scored a goal.

I am smiling but when I open my eyes the table is empty, and I am alone. There is a big horse painted on the wall by James and even some old sketch books of Kitty's with the box of watercolours, and it was only Easter they sat there and today it's autumn with the leaves falling outside.

I walk to the window and press my face against the glass. The garden is overgrown. Wild clumps of tufty grass reclaiming once neatly trimmed lawns. The wind is picking up the leaves and twirling them about. I open the window and the breeze blows in. I can hear the wood pigeons calling from the trees. A few leaves still cling to the twigs.

What has happened in that time, from spring to autumn, the lifetime of a leaf? What happened when it poked its way through the four small doors, and unfurled its pale-green folded-up pleats to the world? James died. And what happened as the yellow green darkened to summer green, then began to turn yellow at the edges as late summer crept along the branches? Kitty died.

Now the leaves are falling.

I have to go outside. I have to be in the garden. I walk through the swing door and down the back stairs, and out the door in the dining room. I run across the grass and into the trees, where the wind is loud in the branches.

I go more slowly up the bank. A large tree has been uprooted by the equinox gales. I sit by the exposed earth, and smell the damp soil. The roots have been ripped out of the ground, there is a pool of red water in the hole. I lie on the damp grass near the hole. I look at the mud clinging to the roots.

James went along to the gun room and took a rifle down from the stand. He must have loaded it at night in the dark, and he lay down outside in the leaves and hugged the gun as though it was a friend.

The long trunk has a green powdery surface. It is a pine tree. The bark has a rich fragrant smell. I turn my face over and smell the grass. I look into the pool of red water, and see the swaying branches reflected from the sky. The sky is white, my reflected face is orange.

'I just can't stand it,' he had said, 'I'm in a vice.'

'But what is it?' and I saw an image in my mind of the monster that swallowed Papa.

'Drugs,' he said. 'Drink.'

I tried to look at the monster, but it was a gaping chasm.

'We need to love ourselves more, that's what it is, you're just not seeing that you're someone with a good heart, you're a loving person. Don't you see how valuable that is?'

He looked at me with faraway eyes.

'Oh you're so nice,' he said and smiled a lame smile, but nothing had penetrated. His heart was heavy and full of dark sad feelings.

'We've got a monster, James. It keeps swallowing us, it's not you.'

'Who is it then?' he said wanly.

But the monster whispered and he went to the gun room, and that's why he lay down in last year's dead leaves just as the new ones were pushing through the twigs, and that's why he pressed the gun to his heart and pulled the trigger. He wanted to go home.

I cry, the tears fall off my face and drop into the red pool. They make little rings on the surface of the water and a tiny plip sound. I wipe them away and get up to wander through the trees and back across the grass to sit under the music-room windows by the copper beech. The dark leaves turn to deep dusty purple when they fall.

I get up from the roots of the copper beech. I can't settle anywhere. My mind runs from one thing to another. I walk along the grass in front of the house and look across to the fountain. It is empty of water and the stone man has disappeared, packed in a square box among straw and sitting in the gun-room passage. I walk back up the dining-room stairs.

The furniture is being packed up for the auction. The chairs stand in rows ready to be taken downstairs. The house will soon be sold. I run along the passage up the back stairs to the old nursery to find refuge from the furniture numbered with cloakroom tickets and standing out from the wall.

I reach the top of the stairs and walk along the corridor into the nursery. I walk across to the open window. The breeze blows in. I can hear the wood pigeons calling from the trees.

Kitty and I lay on a bed in a hotel with the window open. I didn't want to leave her, even go out of the room. I didn't want to be anywhere without her, and feel all the feelings about James on my own. So we lay together on the bed, with our bare arms wrapped around each other, letting the terrible feelings pass through us at the same time, and outside we could hear the sea lapping against the rocks and the seagulls calling plaintive cries in the air. They called through us, and the sound felt our pain.

I look down at the orchard. White blossom falls like snow at the beginning of summer. Now the branches are naked and reach into the sky.

'You wouldn't do that too, would you, Kitty?'

She gets up on her elbows, she knows what I mean.

'No, I wouldn't. It's not something I'm going to do, all right?'

I nod, I smile.

'You wouldn't either, would you?'

'No, I promise.'

We give each other a hug.

But I left her there and said goodbye from the train. She went swimming and was pulled under by the currents of a foreign sea. I am as naked as the branches without her.

I walk away from the window and sit on a chair. I watch the sky in the dimming light. I want to be here and sit very still. I want to hear the vibration of a faraway sound. Because I know where they have gone. I can feel it in my dreams. Not with Papa in the church across the fields. Not there.

And I can't think of Kitty's terrified struggle for life, and I can't think of the pain that made James pull the trigger, because I can feel where they have gone. It is a singing place full of light. It dazzles me. I long for the sweetness of it.

It is home, and I want to go home.

Oh no, I am not sad that they have gone. I am sad that they have gone without me.

And from deep inside me a child cries out, 'Take me with you, please can't I come? Don't leave me in this cold place alone.'

P auline has built a fire in the grate, and when the grown-ups come up from downstairs the nursery smells of coal and toast.

We stand up when they come in. Mama is with a lady with red hair and an orange hairband, who says, 'Ah, how lovely, nursery tea.'

'Darling, come and say hello to Lady Peters.'

I shake the lady's hand and make a little bob. I have been changed into my velvet dress for tea and my patent-leather shoes hurt.

'This is my fourth, Mary Elizabeth.'

'How do you do.'

Papa stands at the window that looks out towards the blue hills and the bottom lawn, the tall green wellingtonia, and the kitchen gardens, and waves his hand across the scene.

'Best view in the house!' he says to the lady's husband, waving his hand across again. 'The house should really face south, towards the view!'

I climb up on to the toy box under the other window that looks down on the fountain, the stone steps and the balustrade that lead to the upper lawn, the cherry orchard and the invisible ha-ha beyond, and wonder what makes a good view and a bad one.

When we are settled at the table Kitty comes rushing in, and nods to the visitors. I can see she has Bumhug up her sleeve, because of his quivering whiskers. When she stretches her arm to the butter dish, the bulge travels up her arm and behind her hair. I notice Lady Peters noticing too.

She turns to me with a look left over from the travelling bulge, and says, 'And do you know when your birthday is?'

I nod, thinking it a strange question, and wait for any others, but she looks unsettled, and I feel sorry for her, so I say, 'Do you know when your birthday is?' and she nods, and smiles, and looks at the table, and my mother says, 'A biscuit, Lady Peters?' and offers her a jam ring. She takes it and looks relieved until she sees that on her plate is a half-eaten egg sandwich. But James announces his birthday and smiles at her and that seems to save her from her trouble and they begin a conversation.

Papa talks and laughs loudly, and we all eat toast and jam and biscuits and sandwiches, and I see Bumhug's long pink tail outside Kitty's collar as he travels down the other arm, and it is time to cut the cake, and I am allowed to keep a pink rose.

I whisper to Doreen, 'Please may I get down?' and she

says yes, and I say my grace, 'Thank you, God, for my good tea, name the Father, Son, and Holy Ghost, Ah! Men,' and do the sign of the cross and Pauline has drawn the curtains and I slip in between the crack into the quiet stillness of the alcove, the place between outside and in.

The curtain has a thin strip of light and the green-and-white stripes dance with the firelight. Outside the sky is getting darker. I press my face up against the window and with cold glass against my cheek attempt to penetrate the shadows in the darkening blue light.

I look across the expanse of grass and into the dark spaces between the quiet trees. Something knows, not me, not them, but something does, and that something penetrates my being with what it knows. It does not tell me, it just says, 'Here is mystery,' and I hold mystery within me untouched.

The Egg was once a staircase, but now it is a vast hole lit by a domed skylight. Only the light does not reach the floor below, but filters in a greenish way around the banisters that surround it.

When the lights are on downstairs I can see the pink carpet with flowers on it, and I would not even know that terror lives in the cold library and seeps up through the Egg, at night, when the lights are out.

I hold Doreen's hand as we pass by, and even James

does not run ahead, past the scowling man with white hair, who follows us from one end of the dark corridor to the other with his black eyes. We screw up our sweetie papers into bullets to throw at the portrait if no one is by.

We reach the top of the stairs, and I greet the gold birds hiding in the black foliage. I lift up my dressing gown and hold the black leaves of the banister and take one step at a time. I have had my bath. Doreen told me that if I didn't clean my ears, potatoes would grow in them. I am so excited by the idea, I have made sure not to clean them. I imagine the potatoes growing up a trellis in a tiny garden in my ears.

Great Aunt Elizabeth peeps out from behind her mother's skirts, and the King of Spain looks down his nose, and the huge brass chandelier drops into the wide-open space on its long chain. I like looking through the leaves to see the black diamond shapes on the hall floor so far far below, and then to the ceiling that stretches up past the windows, to the huge circle of little white flowers.

We reach the landing and walk along the honey-coloured carpet to the sitting-room door. Doreen knocks.

'Come in!' says a singing voice.

We enter. It is a cosy, warm room, full of big comfortable armchairs, geraniums, and books. There is a white sheepskin rug in front of the log fire. The air is lit with yellow lights and smells of juniper.

Mama sits in a large blue armchair with her sewing.

'Hello, darlings!' she coos. She nods to Doreen. 'Thank you, that's all.'

'Aren't you smart in your new pyjamas!'

Mama puts her sewing to one side and makes a space for us to kneel by her feet so we can say our prayers to her.

We kneel down, and clasp our hands. She has black crocodile-skin shoes, with a gold chain across that clinks when she walks along. Like a flower she has her own fragrance, sweet and a little spicy, everything that touches her becomes one with it, even her blue stockings. On her lap her long fingers hold each other, but the joints are big so the rings are loose and they rattle up and down.

She is wearing a blue, pink and white striped blouse, an ornate cross hangs in the folds. She has pink lips, and a nose with a tilted tip, and a little wart on the side. It is called a white mole.

Her eyes are cast downwards to her fingers. Beneath the skin of the lids, I can see blue veins.

We say our prayers. 'Hail Mary, full of grace,' which means Hello, Mama, full of a kind of brown rice (which is chewy), 'Blessed is the froop of thy womb Jesus.' A froop is a small trumpet they blow around the baby's head. 'Holy Mary, Mother of God,' shows Mama wearing a crown of flowers, on the top of a great hill, and 'Pray for us sinners,' entreats her to pray for all the insects and snails, James and

I among them, who live at its foot. 'Now and at the hour of our death,' conjures a deep resounding cavern within me full of the unknown.

There are many statues and pictures of Mama and the baby all over the house, sometimes in her blue cloak, that she wears on Sundays to the big church.

In the secret garden, above the aspidistra, there is her likeness in stone. I sit beside her sometimes on the wall, when we crawl under the poison berries to jump into the piles of dead leaves Callum has raked up from the lawn. I put my arms around her and the baby, but not for too long because the stone is cold. Her cheek is smooth and her eyes without pupils look down tenderly. I blow my cold smoky breath into her ear.

Mama clears her throat and we say words to the Angel of God, My Guardian Dear. It is a green and gold prayer, and every feather is outlined with yellow threads.

Mama puts her glasses back on and lifts up her sewing. There is a knock on the door and Doreen has arrived to take us back upstairs. Mama puts her cheek out to be kissed.

Junket is a milky bluish pink. It trembles. Tapioca is like frogspawn with the tadpoles not yet hatched. It slithers down your throat. I look at the two round bowls for pudding and back to my plate. I look from the mince to the orange turnip. Hugh has his mashed up in the mincer and it comes out all one colour. I'd like that, then I wouldn't know it was turnip. Babies don't know. I have seen Annie being given raw liver to eat. Doreen chops it up and feeds it to her, just like Kitty feeding the kestrel who sits on her finger and swallows, blinking upwards with blue-grey lids. I try to mash mine up like Hugh's.

'Elizabeth, stop playing with your food.'

We sit around the big square nursery table. I watch the grey clouds pass in the bright white sky outside.

'James, I've told you before.'

James looks up from his plate. He is making furrows in his mince and planting the peas. He turns his lower lip over backwards and frowns so Kitty and I laugh.

'Stop acting up, James!'

He raises his eyebrows and crosses his eyes. Doreen ignores him. Tears are welling up behind my glasses in an effort not to laugh. Doreen gets up and leaves the room to fetch the water jug from the pantry. I seize my chance and jump down from my chair, run to the handkerchiefs, and climb back up, put the orange turnip in the hankie, and leave it on my lap. My hands trembling, I pick up my knife and fork and, as Doreen returns, hurry to swallow what is left on my plate.

'Mary Elizabeth, where is your turnip?'

'I've eaten it,' I whisper.

The others look down at their plates.

'Stand up!'

I stand up and the turnip falls to the floor in its hanky which has left a stain of turnip juice on my skirt.

'You naughty, lying girl!' She holds my hand in hers, and gives a smack for each word. I look away into the bright grey clouds and what I see blurs as the space between my eyes and my glasses fills up with water so I think it must be like this seeing from inside a goldfish bowl and I look at the goldfish just to check, swimming with his multi-coloured stones and one plant, round and round.

'Look at me when I'm talking to you,' says Doreen, and I look at her through my water blur.

'Go to bed, right this minute.'

I get in between the cold sheets in the night nursery with its carpet of grass. The blinds of both windows are drawn, but I can see a small crack of sky. I lie watching the crack.

We walk behind the large black creaking pram. The rain has filled the potholes with puddles and turned the pebbles mauve. I can smell the gooseberry leaves in the wet air.

My glasses have got steamed up in the drizzle.

'You should get a pair of windscreen wipers,' says James, and splashes into a puddle.

'Don't you dare get those trousers dirty,' says Doreen, stopping the pram and turning round.

'Where would I get them from?'

'Walk in front where I can see you,' says Doreen.

We walk in front of the pram by the kitchen-garden wall and past the potting shed and through the dark trees.

'Oh, a shop!'

'How do you turn them off, though?' I say, taking my glasses off and trying to wipe them on the sleeve of my damp jersey.

James starts running down the hill past Mrs McCloud's house.

'Don't you climb that gate, James Francis, don't you dare climb that gate!' Doreen shouts from behind.

I run down the hill after James to the gate of Gypsy's field.

'Eeaw,' she brays, and it sounds sad, as though she wrenches it from within her. James climbs up the rungs and leans over the gate.

'Get down from there! Get down right now!'

I put my hand through the rungs and stroke Gypsy's soft nose and pat her neck, and look into her deep brown eyes.

James gets down from the gate.

'Let's do an ambush,' he says.

'Yeah, let's do an ambush.'

I don't know what it is, but I follow James down the stony track, past the stables.

'Come back, you two. Where do you think you're going? Come back this instant!'

I suppose it will be all right when she knows it is because we are doing an ambush.

'Come back right now!'

I follow James. We run round the tower, and through the stone quadrangle where horses used to clatter, past the carriage house, and climb the gate to squat behind the thin limbs of the box hedge which cannot possibly hide us, and wait for Doreen to pass by.

I am hoping it will all turn out all right, James is giggling the help-we're-in-trouble giggle. As she passes I follow James's lead and spring out with the Indian war cry, running round and round the pram in a circle. Doreen stands with her hands on her hips and her mouth a thin line.

'We ambushed you!' says James.

'I'll ambush you!' says Doreen, catching on to his wrist and smacking his bottom. 'You are not to run away like that! Do you hear? And you too, madam.' My wrist is caught, my bottom smacked.

'Do as you are told!'

We lag behind now.

'Doesn't hurt anyway with my duffel coat,' says James.

*   *   *

It is on the way back from our walk, when I feel the something that creeps secretly under the ground, and silently up the tree trunks and along the branches to turn the colour of the leaves. It stirs and awakens me to the presence of an unknown invisible world as I walk through the grass and the lying leaves, with the trees aflame, and the sun low in the sky casting long blue shadows between the glowing strips of light.

'Come here. What are you doing wandering about?' Doreen calls me back to the pram.

I look up and see a man with large eyes smiling from the green and yellow leaves of a tall beech tree. I stop to smile at him. The wind blows and he throws his head back and laughs and laughs.

'We haven't got all day, you know.'

A bird flies out of his eye.

She comes across the grass, catches my hand, and pulls me to the pram.

'Honestly, sometimes I wonder if you're all there behind those glasses.'

I look at her for a moment. I too have wondered this.

I look for his face again in the sunlit trees at the edge of the field. Today the air is still and cold, and full of light. There is frost on the plough. In the distance the trees turn blue, but the tall beeches nearby are glowing yellow and orange. The tips of my fingers and toes nip with cold. I can see my breath.

There is a beating and a fluttering from the woods and a crowd of pheasants flies over in a rush. Papa drops my hand and lifts the gun to his shoulder, following the birds above his head. Crack! Bang! There is a whizzing sound, the smell of gunpowder, the birds fall with a thud in two places. Shots crack the air across the field. The pheasants cry out. The men shout, 'Good shot, sir!' The flurry ceases. The dogs are sent to fetch the birds. A rabbit convulses in the stubble. Mr McPhail picks him up and breaks the neck. I flinch, getting myself mixed up with the rabbit.

The rowan trees are heavy with berries and hang over the fence. We climb back into the Land Rover. Mr McPhail's plus fours smell of moss.

The pheasants are lined up in rows on the lawn at the front. Tall men stand in groups wearing shooting socks of beautiful colours, deep green, rust, burgundy, and pale morning sky blue. The rabbit's eyes have clouded. The brilliant emerald sheen of the pheasants lights up in the sun. Mr McPhail counts how many are dead.

In the scullery the birds are stacked up in front of the square table. Mrs McCloud stands on the platform by the two stone sinks, and the rabbits lie in a pile at her feet. She is a hilly landscape all to herself, covered in blue forget-me-nots. Her white hair is tied back from her face. She plucks away with such gentle movements and so rhythmically, it looks easy. The feathers blow about in the air and float up our noses when we breathe in. I watch as she slices open the body of the bird, and reaches in to tenderly scoop out the purple clots of blood and pale-pink glistening strings of guts. She washes the bird inside and out until it is clean, and places it on the side. She looks down at me near her elbow. Her eyes are deep and full of light, there is a world inside her eyes. I walk in. Mr McCloud is standing in a grass field that slopes down into a valley. Mrs McCloud smiles, and washes her hands under the tap and dries them on her apron.

'Now then, Master James, which is your rabbit?'

James is loitering near the door, reluctant to come near the smell of blood. He shrugs.

'Don't know. He just said I had to gut one, seeing as I shot it, I have to gut it.'

'Look now,' she says beckoning him closer to the window, and picking a rabbit from the pile, 'stand at the sink, there's a good lad.'

It is gloomy in the scullery. Mrs McCloud stands in the gloom, white-haired and blue-skied, letting in the sunlight, and holding James's rabbit in her soft round hands.

James sidles around the table to stand beside her under the window. She puts the rabbit down on the sideboard. James's hands screw each other together behind his back. His head is tilted to one side, only half looking at the rabbit.

'Are ye scunnered?' asks Mrs McCloud. James nods.

'Och, ma Jim wid be too!'

'Now.' She lays the rabbit on its side and slits it from tip to tail with her sharp knife.

James's face is screwed up, only catching the rabbit sideways on. Mrs McCloud keeps looking at him and having a little giggle.

'Och, it's no sae bad, we're only going to take his coat off.'

That's no good to James – as the greenish entrails slide out of the slit with clots of purple blood and guts filled with rabbit pellets, he turns white, then pale green and wretches into the sink with the guts. Nothing comes out but he can't stop wretching until Mrs McCloud guides him over to the other sink and runs the water to splash his face and get him away from the smell and sight of the guts. He sits down on the side of a chair by the towel rail, his face is pale and damp. He keeps closing his eyes and swallowing.

'Just like ma Jim!' says Mrs McCloud half to herself, shaking her head and giggling.

*　　*　　*

I wait and listen in the doorway of the scullery.

Doreen and Pauline are having a cup of tea and a blether with Mrs Fergus at the small table, by the tall window that looks on to the back yard and the green house on stilts.

The echoing walls of the kitchen stretch up and the sunlight streams down from the high windows near the ceiling.

'He carried twenty sacks! Twenty sacks from the coal lorry!' Doreen is saying.

'Along that corridor, then every one into the lift. I don't know how many trips he made up to the nursery cellar, his back was breaking after it, and he got his thanks in a nutshell!'

Mrs Fergus shakes her head. They are all fond of Doreen's brother. I am interested by the nutshell and wonder how you get the thanks in.

'It's beyond me,' she says, looking aghast.

But I look into the nutshell and see that it is empty, and then I understand that hauling sack after sack of coal, for an empty walnut, is no good at all.

Pauline looks out on the yard, towards the blue hills, and I wonder if she is following the coal lorry all the way to England.

Michael was covered in soot, when Pauline and I went to offer him tea and a biscuit. He had black hands and a black face, but his eyes shone with light when he looked at Pauline. It made her blush. Perhaps he would have hauled the coal, sack by sack, all the way back down the stairs again if Pauline had been there to see him do it.

Mrs Cowe is oiling snipe with her red fingers and piercing them with their own beaks.

'Walls have ears,' she announces, looking at the others but nodding towards me.

I look quickly up at the white tiles stretching up to the ceiling to see if I can see them.

'Och, she's quiet as a wee mouse!'

'Kitty didn't have a quiet mouse,' I suggest to Doreen as we take the lift back up to the nursery.

'Well, he's quiet now!' says Doreen abruptly, 'and we'll hear no more about it.'

Kitty's mouse escaped, and fell down the lift shaft. She picked up his pink-and-white flattened body in her long slender fingers, and we buried him in the moat, where snowdrops would grow over him.

I am already walking across the night nursery in my bare feet, when I wake up and notice I am following Clementina and James into the corridor, and being guided by whispers.

The nursery is dark. The nannies are downstairs. We

creep around the Egg, and look through the wooden pillars. Light blazes from beneath. Sounds of laughing float up from the drawing room. Mrs McCready opens a tall door below us, and we watch her cross the floor with a tray of clinking glasses.

The house hums with a gentle pleasure when the rooms are lit up and there is activity in its many corners.

A door opens along the corridor, and we creep towards the stripy room to spy an enormous tulip waft down the stairs leaving the air scented with lilies. Through the banisters I watch her red-edged petals float up and down.

We crouch behind the black foliage in our pyjamas.

'James, you bring up the rear.'

'Why've I got to bring up the rear?' James complains.

'She'll get lost somewhere and give us away, that's why, and it wasn't my idea to bring her.'

He shrugs.

'Right then, I want us to take it fast across the saloon, but we'll have to go past the drawing-room door, one by one. So, wait for my command!'

As one body we move down the stairs and through the double doors of the saloon. The shimmering chandelier with its thousand glass droplets tinkles gently as we move across the floor.

We duck down beside the black lion's feet of a tall gold-

and-black cane chair. Papa says not to sit on these chairs. 'They are very old, very delicate, and very precious!'

I never would, I think to myself. There's nearly always someone already sitting there.

James pokes me from behind. 'Your turn,' he whispers.

I scuttle past the open door of the drawing room, filled with gold lights and brilliant flowers, and join the others behind the chest outside the morning room.

Clementina signals to us from the dining-room door.

'All clear,' she whispers, and motions us to join her.

The dining room flickers quietly in the light of a hundred candles. They reflect in the glasses, and the glass droplets that hang from the candlesticks. They twinkle in the long rows of knives and forks, the silver salt and pepper cellars, the white plates edged with blue and gold. I slip behind a long red curtain and look at the dark garden in pale-blue moonlight. The trees are still. The garden is dreaming. Its mysterious dream fills me with quietness. I poke my head back into the gentle yellow candlelight.

Suddenly there are footsteps coming from the pantry. Clementina lifts up the white tablecloth.

'Quick! Underneath!'

I dive under, knocking my head. James and Kitty follow. I sit watching strange sparks popping before my eyes.

Mrs McCready and Mrs McKay are bringing in the soup. They arrange it on the hotplate.

James clasps his hand over his mouth when we hear the rumble of many footsteps and chirruping voices making its way towards the door, and we look at each other's pale faces in the glimmering light when we hear the door opening and Mama's high voice saying, 'Major, do sit by me, darling Antonia, would you like to take John's right,' and we watch in cool horror as the walls of the long white house are punctuated by many pairs of shoes.

James and Kitty begin to giggle uncontrollably. James holds his nose to stop it but only succeeds in snorting which makes them laugh more. Clementina looks unusually bewildered. I crawl along to sit in the comforting presence of Papa's long shoes.

Something tells him I am there, and a big hand feels its way under the cloth carrying some curly toast, awkwardly buttered. I take the toast and crunch it. The big hand feels around for my head and gives my hair a stroke. I give the hand a few small pats, and it strokes my cheek.

After some time, and plenty of loud talking and laughter above our heads, the big hand lifts up the cloth, and beckons us with its forefinger. We follow one another quietly from under the table, and crawl across the floor. The door to the pantry is open, and once through, we run up the back stairs and don't stop until we are past the swing door and into the nursery corridor.

My feet are cold and dirty from the black back stairs, but my bed is still warm when I climb back in, and return to my own dream.

Between green legs and a black gear stick with a red knob that rattles, I sit uncomfortably. The Land Rover smells of diesel and roars so the grown-ups shout at each other over my head. The sky is white. The Land Rover bumps and rattles, and stops at last.

We get out and I am surrounded by the different-coloured legs. Pale orange, moss green and indigo, held up by scarlet flashes. The nailed boots make scraping sounds on the road. I dodge the shining barrels of guns. The dogs are excited and their long pink tongues hang out as they pant, and the spit falls on the road.

I am lifted over the fence and into the tall heather. I hold Papa's hand as we walk through it. Sometimes he lifts me off the ground by my hand. The heather is bouncy and I fall down invisible holes. Then we see the flat silver loch in the distance, glinting like an eye at the sky.

When we reach the side of the water we are told to crouch in the reeds. I look at the round rosettes stuck to the side of their long stems.

James comes to sit by me and whispers, 'We're going to see the falling leaf, Specky.'

'Oh.'

'They've come all the way from Iceland.'

'Who have?'

'The pink-foot!'

'Oh good.'

A dog is panting beside me. I can see his breath. The surface of the water has little ripples as the wind blows across it, and it makes gentle lapping sounds as it touches the reeds. We are all quiet, surrounding the loch, except for whispers and someone sneezing.

We wait. It begins to get chilly. James and I huddle together and rub our hands. Still we wait as the sky turns from white to grey to a clear pale blue.

Then in the far-off distance we hear them. 'Wa-wa, wa-wa.'

The sound gets louder, we sit waiting.

Then in a great rush, we see them. They are coming from two directions, flying in long skeins. I hold my breath in wonder. They join, and fly above our heads around the loch. More and more arrive until the air is thrumming with their beating wings and calling voices. All at once, as though they have agreed it, there is a hush, and in the strange and sudden silence, against the twilit sky, I see hundreds of geese with the air whirring through their outstretched wings, falling out of the sky in the shape of a vast falling leaf.

'It's the falling leaf!' whispers James.

'The falling leaf!' I say.

A rifle cracks the silence. The sound echoes off the loch. Then all the guns are banging, and a cascade of shot shivers into the water. Geese are flying in all directions, splashing dead into the water, or thudding on to the bank. I begin to whine, and the dog next to me whines also.

'Quiet!' says the keeper, 'you can wait to fetch 'em.'

It comes to an end abruptly and the dogs are sent to fetch the floating bodies. I feel an empty coldness fill my belly. My legs do not work as I try to stand. It is dark now.

Conversations about good shot, and see that one go down! linger above my head as I try to address the problem of legs, heather and the darkness, and something in my throat I can't swallow. James gets hold of a flask of whisky mac.

'Here, have a swig.'

I do so and it melts everything inside me and warms me up. I take another and the sweet ginger makes my mouth water and I take another. I bound up and over the heather. It is a long walk home. I ask to be carried by various uncles and take swigs from as many flasks as I can find. I fall down holes and bounce carelessly into gullies and over hills. I am filled with warmth and a sense of boundlessness. When I reach the road, among the breeched and stockinged legs, the smell of gunpowder and wet dogs, I am completely drunk.

I sit behind Papa in the Land Rover on the way home. I pull his hat off and call him John. He laughs.

'You're sloshed, Lizzie!'

'Sloshed, schloshed!' I sing.

We arrive home, I am vaguely aware of being carried along by two people either side. It is Kitty and James, they are taller than me and it is uncomfortable under my armpits. They are laughing because my feet don't seem to touch the ground.

Mama comes down the stairs. Through increasing blur I see a stony face. The air turns cold.

'Hello, Mary, I'm schloshed!' I slur, hoping to brighten her up.

'Pull yourself together,' says an icy voice. I feel the sting of a slap on my face.

The next thing I know I wake up in my parents' bedroom with an extraordinary headache that pounds through my whole body, and a feeling of weakness and immense shame.

In the days that follow my shame creeps inside me and floats about in the corners of the nursery. I feel choked by it. I cannot look at anyone and Clementina delights in chanting 'Drunk! Drunk!'

The sheer terror of sitting at Mama's knee at prayer time is almost unbearable, and I keep my eyes tightly closed and pray fervently to be forgiven, only to see her face rising in my mind and hissing, 'Pull yourself together!'

The invisible beings of the house seem to draw closer to me and I feel their shadows passing through me. Little winds blow in my ear, and make me shiver, and strange wispy feelings slide up and down my spine. Then one morning, a miracle happens.

We see it first, shining in the crack under the blind. A different light comes from the garden when Doreen pulls back the curtains in the night nursery. She draws up the blinds and we see that it is a snow light. Everything is white. The man playing his pipes in the fountain is cloaked in snow, and the water is frozen. The lawns are pure untroubled whiteness, brighter than the sky. Each branch and twig is outlined, the bushes are capped in snow, and the stone benches are hidden beneath drifts. The flakes continue to fall silently.

The snow light fills our minds with wide white spaces, it dazzles our thoughts, and we breathe new air.

*   *   *

Suddenly the house is entering a new era.

Preparations are happening in all its corners. Mr McKay and Callum bring swags and hang them in loops along the banisters, filling the stairway and every landing with the juicy scent of evergreens and berries.

Stuart brings a gigantic tree that has to be hoisted from the trailer with ropes up on to the balcony and through the double doors of the saloon to stand in splendour in front of the windows shining a magnificent dark-green presence into the house. Holly and mistletoe and glittering strings of dancing shapes are hung from pictures and mirrors and around lights.

Mrs Cowe and Mrs Fergus are busy stirring great puddings and baking pastries, and Mrs McCloud is peeling mountains of potatoes for the house has filled with unknown people and other children, and they all must be fed.

Fires are lit in usually empty rooms and beds made up, bathrooms along deserted corridors fill up with steam and the scent of lavender water. Sounds of rejoicing float on the air.

'Tell me again, Granny.' The room is warm and full of twinkling lights. 'Tell me again.'

Her face is a lilac sky. A soft wind of heather blows from her mouth. She takes me on the wind to a moonlit wood and the tall trees are black against the sky. Little Granny is gathering sticks, a cloud passes across the face of the moon and little Granny is frightened. 'Mona!' she whispers. 'Ssht!' says the older girl. They are going to build a nest in the treetops and wait till the fairies come. She has climbed out her bedroom window and she is fearful lest her father finds her, more fearful still of those naughty night goblins that like to trick you . . . I stand in the forest with her, my eyes trying to penetrate the darkness and catch a glimpse of the fairies for myself, but the dark undergrowth turns into the lilac sky, and a voice from the sky says, 'Elizabeth!' I focus my eyes into its brightness and see Granny's face smiling.

'Ah! There now we have you back. I'll tell you the rest of the story another time. You're to choose your stocking now.'

'Choose stockings, then sing carols!' says Mama, who lets a pile of Papa's shooting socks fall on to the sheepskin rug in front of the bright flames. I reluctantly leave my bed of heather and sidle towards the pile. The sitting room is filled with people I have never seen before. Clementina pounces on the deep Prussian blue.

'Bags it!' she yells.

I begin to be interested in the colours. James chooses a bright-red one, and Kitty a green like the moss that grows by the burn. There is deep red, sky blue that belongs to Hugh. Grey pink is the one I choose for myself.

'Everyone chosen?' says Mama's high voice.

'Yes,' says Clementina, 'and I've got the best one!'

'No you haven't,' says James.

'Blue is better than re-ed, blue is better than re-ed,' chants Clementina.

'Crap!' shouts James.

'James, please,' says Mama and looks at him with her hard eye. He hangs his head under her gaze.

'Let's all be nice, and come and sing carols.'

We troop through the door. The striped sofa by the stairs is piled high with presents. The banisters tied with swags fill the air with the scent of juicy evergreen stems and holly. In the pale-orange saloon the tall tree almost touches the white garlands that curl around on the ceiling.

Papa has long long sticks with tapers on the end.

'Oh, can I?' says Clementina.

He hands her one and distributes others among the children. He picks me up into his green arms and puts the long taper in my hand and lights it from the flames that leap up the wide chimney. Holding around my hand we stretch up to the tallest candles on the tree. I gasp as he stretches and light up as each candle flickers alight. We stride around the tree making sure that each curling red candle has a light dancing above it. The pine mingles with the smell of wax. Mama turns out the chandelier. The huge room flickers, and the shining balls on the Christmas tree are alive in the night.

Papa lets me down. I am a small person again.

We gather around the glimmering alcove where the Nativity is set up among straw, and we sing about the sky filled with angels, and bells ringing, and kings on horseback from a golden city, and a little town, and endless stars, and a baby's sweet head. And in the glowing darkness, an atmosphere of hidden joy spreads among us, for we have entered into a mysterious union with the spirit of Christmas, and when the lights are turned on and the candles blown out or extinguished with sponges on the same long sticks, the spirit is still glimmering in our eyes.

The presents are arranged in piles beneath the tree. The white snow light shines through the windows. The flames leap in the tall fireplace which we take turns to stand inside, until we're told not to because it's dangerous, but James does it anyway so we call him James Flames.

The grown-ups stand around murmuring. Their presents are on the stone table or black-and-gold cane chairs. They do not jump on them as we do, but pretend that presents are nothing at all to get excited about. The stone table has wooden legs carved in the shape of a lion with its tongue sticking out. My eye travels up the lion and on to the marble table top to Mama's pile. My present to her is wrapped in pink tissue paper and is third down on her pile. It is a book of pictures, that Pauline helped me to stitch together. It says her name on the front.

I open my presents slowly, keeping an eye on Mama as she tantalisingly hovers about, half opening a present, then going to be kissed for a gift.

In a bright package of blue paper and silver stars, I find a torch that changes colour when you turn the face. It has batteries and works straightaway. I understand how to work it, and see that I can change the colour of the light from green to red to blue to yellow. I put the red light up to my eyes and feel filled with its warmth. I try shining the yellow light into just one eye, and when I take it away the world looks different through each eye. I hold the green light up to my eyes, and blink very fast.

'Elizabeth, it's for seeing in the dark!' a helpful grown-up calls to me. 'You're supposed to shine it the other way!' and they laugh, but I turn to Mama and she is unwrapping my present and I nearly missed it and I can't see very well because my eyes are filled with after-green light, and blinking, I see her take off the pink tissue paper, only now it looks dark blue, and blinking again I see her finding my book stitched up the spine, and still trying to blink away the purple blobs that are floating about in my vision, I watch as she lays it to one side and does not read it or open it, or even turn it over, but turns to pick up her next present, and I find the blue face of the torch and lying down on my back under the tree, which smells so green, I look for a long time with both eyes wide open into the glowing face of the blue light.

We are sitting on the black sheepskin rug in front of the nursery fireguard eating oranges for supper. The sticky juice is all over my fingers and round my mouth. James and I have had our bath and we are in our pyjamas. The coal fire has burst up into flame. Mrs McCready is sitting on the green sofa knitting, while Doreen and Pauline take turns to clomp across the red linoleum in platform sandals to check what they look like in the nursery mirror. They are going out to the Dinner Dance.

When Pauline came back from her shopping she un-wrapped the new sandals from folded yellow tissue paper and took them out of the box. They weren't suede, she said, but you'd never know. She put them on the dressing table one at a time for me to admire. Then she put them on the floor, for me to try on. They had red straps, and sling-backs.

When I put them on I was nearly as tall as Pauline, only Doreen came in and gave me a smack and said I'd break my ankle if I tried that again. When she went out the room, Pauline let me try her frosted-mint eye-shadow, sitting up at the dressing table, but not to colour in my cheeks with it, because you had to use blusher for that. She showed me a picture in a magazine of a woman with blonde curls, and a billowing white dress in a misty field of buttercups. She was wearing frosted-mint eye-shadow. Pauline said she would like a perm like hers but her hair is dark and straight so she had a feather-cut. I told her I liked the feather-cut best.

The radio in the nursery plays, 'Like a bridge over troubled waters, I will lay me down,' and I think of the wooden sheep bridge at the bottom of the hill to Mr McPhail's house. When the burn is in spate the water turns dark and frothy, and slips along in roaring water snakes. Kitty and James built a dam there once, and the spate water washed it clean away.

'D'ye like ma maxi, James?' says Pauline turning to look at him.

James looks up and shrugs his shoulders.

'What's she talking about?' he whispers to me.

Pauline stands in front of the mirror in a long apricot dress, it has frills around the hem and around the neck and a velvet ribbon sewed into a bow under her bosoms. She turns around to look at herself from behind, and smooths her dress down.

Before Pauline there was Marion. She had a shiny forehead, and pointed bosoms that came through her jersey like darts. James and I were so intrigued by her pointed bosoms that we climbed up on to the hot pipes in the nursery pantry to look through the window into the bathroom to see Marion in the bath and catch sight of them. But the glass was pale green and wiggly and even with our faces pressed up against the glass it was impossible to make out anything at all. Only it was obvious from the other side because Marion screamed and Doreen found us up there. We didn't have oranges that night, or hot Ribena, and had to go straight to bed after a smacking.

I throw my orange skin on to the fire and the flames spit and hiss.

Doreen looks at the clock. 'For crying out loud, is that the time?'

'Kitty, are you ready?' she shouts through the nursery door, and turns to Mrs McCready. 'That lassy dawdles!'

'Go and tell Kitty to hurry, they'll be going through in a minute!' she says to me and motions with her thumb, 'and wash that juice off your hands!' she shouts after me.

Kitty is sitting on her bed swinging her legs back and forth. When I come in she takes her thumb out of her mouth because she's too old to suck her thumb. 'A girl your age!' said Aunt Winnie.

She is dressed in her blue dress with the large white collar and red tie.

'Doreen says are you ready?'

She nods. I climb up beside her on to the bed.

'Don't you want to have dinner in the dining room?'

38

She shakes her head.

'Why not?'

Silence.

'Clementina likes it, I think.'

'Clementina likes talking to people.'

'Don't you?'

Kitty puts her thumb back in and shakes her head. Then takes it out again and says, 'I don't know what to say.'

'But you get pudding!' Dining-room puddings are elaborate, brandy-snap coffee cups filled with cream, little cakes in the shape of peacocks, crystallised primroses, trellis baskets made from icing sugar, these are the specialities of Mrs Fergus.

Kitty sighs. 'I don't like eating when I can't think of what to say.'

'I'll wave when you go through to dinner. I'll watch over the Egg.'

'OK,' she smiles. 'I'll wave back.'

When Pauline and Doreen have hurried through the swing door and down the back stairs, and Kitty has reluctantly walked along the corridor and down the front stairs, James and I go and stand by the Egg and look through the gaps in the wooden balustrade. Mrs McCready looks over the ledge between the pillars. We wait. There is a stirring from the drawing room, and the sound of laughing and murmuring voices as the door is opened, and the crowd begins to gather and walk from the drawing room, through the saloon, under the Egg and into the dining room. The ladies come first and laugh and chat together. I catch sight of Mama, and Kitty seems little among the sparkling dresses. She looks up and waves.

They pass underneath us and then the men come through in their dark suits, talking in deep voices. The door of the dining room closes and we can't hear them any more.

James and I run through into the night nursery. Tonight the fire is lit and we can watch the flames flicker until our eyes close, and even with your eyes shut you can see the flames dance and smell the wood and there is not one ghost who would dare to enter into that warm flame light. Ghosts like the cold and the dark and the terrors of emptiness. The firelight flickers them away, and when we are cosy and tucked up in bed we watch the flames flicker on the ceiling.

'Do you like the fire?'

'Yes, 'cause it keeps the ghosts away.'

'That's what I was thinking. Do you want to have dinner downstairs?'

'Not likely.'

'Why not?'

'All that dressing up!'

Even Papa has to dress up, put on a dinner jacket and slippers made of tapestry.

'Then you have to sit there and be polite to people. Be all right for you, you could talk to a man, but I'd have to talk to one of those stupid ladies, in all those dresses and earrings, and they'd laugh and say, "Oh you're so sweet," and probably try and kiss me or something.'

Suddenly we hear a whimper from Annie's cot.

'Oh no,' says James, 'I hope she's not going to cry.'

When Annie first arrived she lay among folds of lace next to Mama's bed in a cot tied with ribbons, and flowing with white muslin, and everyone leant over to breathe in her honeycomb scent. But then she came up to the night nursery, her glory over, and lay in the cot with wooden bars around. Sometimes she cries such a long sad cry that James and I take it in turns to climb in beside her to stroke her soft black furry hair and hot cheek.

She begins to whimper and then to cry.

'I'll go,' says James and climbs out of his bed, runs across the floor, climbs up on to Doreen's bed and leaps over into the cot.

'Shshshsh,' he soothes her, 'it's all right, Annie.'

The door opens a crack.

'James! Quick!' I say.

It is Mrs McCready.

'Is the wa'en crying, hen?' she asks.

'Yes,' I say.

'Och. I'll jist lift her fer a moment.'

'Doreen never does,' says James from inside the cot.

'She disne? And whit are you doin' in there, son?'

James climbs out, and runs into the sliver of light the door has opened up and does an impish dance, then leaps into bed.

Mrs McCready has Annie nestled in her huge bosom saying, 'Ma wee lamb, ma pet, ma little darlin,' and Annie is soon asleep.

When the tree is cast out over the balcony and bounces on to the ground outside, and when it looks so much smaller lying down than it did standing up, we know that the light of the Christmas era has begun to fade.

We stand in front of the Christmas tree's crackling flames and watch the gold wrapping paper curl up and burn with blue fire, and the swags once so green and juicy are thrown on with the rest and spit and hiss, as the last of the juice turns to steam.

A harsh icy wind cuts our faces, when we turn away from the flames, and away from the heat the long-lying snow has a frozen crust that breaks at every step. We enter a new season. It is the season of black ice.

We turn away from the fire, and I follow James through the side door into the gun room. There we find his brand-new air rifle, with a red ribbon still tied around the trigger.

After some target practice with the black-and-white cardboard targets pinned to the copper beech tree in the garden, I get bored and cold, because I don't like holding the gun when it kicks into my shoulder and gives me a fright. I chase off to get the toy machine-gun so we can play at ambush and go exploring.

The air is clear and cold but the sun is shining and glistening the frosted branches. We walk along the ridge among the stalks that poke through the snow, because the road is slippy with ice. The valley is white and the burn runs along, in some places iced over.

I have my gloves on but my hands are cold.

We carefully climb down the bank and slide and slip to the bottom. When we reach the rhododendrons, we play at ambushing. I hide behind a tree and jump out. Aka-kakakak, goes the machine gun. James falls down dead, careful not to damage his new gun. Then we swap and he ambushes me. Akakakakak. I fall down in the snow, and lie looking up at the blue sky and naked trees.

I get tired of always playing boy's games, but the time I brought Susan to play, she got guillotined and when I dug her up, her eyes wouldn't shut because of the mud.

'Get up! You'll catch pneumonia!' says James.

He takes out a target and balances it on a tree, and doesn't manage to hit anything at all.

'Well, that's not a bull's eye!'

'Practice makes perfect,' says James.

'I'm cold,' I moan. The wind is chilling my back that got wet in the snow.

'It's your fault, for lying down so long. I told you!'

'Well, let's play!'

'OK then. You run away, I'll come and track you. Go up to the pond, and then you can ambush.'

I run through the twiggy trees and up the hill towards Mr McPhail's house. I can hear the gun dogs barking, and James carries on with his target practice. I run up to a beech and hide behind its tall grey trunk. I see James coming through the trees in his brown anorak, and double back on myself to jump out and surprise him. I stand behind a ridgy barked oak tree. My heart is beating fast, and my hands are trembling, I am going to really surprise him. He comes closer and I stalk up to a nearer tree, I know he doesn't know that I am here waiting. He thinks I am further ahead, he thinks I am up by the pond by now. When he is near, I leap out, and do the war cry, the machine gun goes akakakakak, James turns round with a startled face and fires the air-gun.

There is a crack. The air behind my eyes lights up with a brilliant spark. For a slow moment my head is filled with light. I hear myself scream. I fall down in the snow, I presume I am dead, but the snow soaks through my trousers and I open my eyes. I see the red blood on the snow. I sit up.

'I thought I was dead,' I say.

James closes his eyes and swallows. He looks off to the other side of the valley. I can see the tears in his eyes that he is hiding from me. He wipes them away.

'Sorry I screamed,' I say, getting up on my elbows.

'It's OK.' His voice is thin and reedy. His face is pale. It looks pale blue next to the snow. I blink to make it change.

'Let's wash the blood off,' he says. His hands are trembling.

We scramble down to the cold burn and splash the freezing water over my face.

'You got a bull's eye that time!' I say, hoping to cheer him. He gives a snorty little laugh.

Blood is pouring down the side of my nose. I bathe it in the ice-cold water. James is breathing fast and his ankles and legs are trembling.

'I thought I'd killed you.'

'Yeah, so did I.'

Luckily James has learnt a new word from the *Eagle Annual* which is 'ricocheted', and bullets did this.

'I think it's ricocheted off!' he says.

I am satisfied with this explanation, until we are walking along the ridge back to the house.

'I *think* it's ricocheted off but you do have a hole in your face.'

I am startled and my heart beats faster. But our main concern is how to hide it from the nannies.

'My glasses come back from the mender's soon, then I could hide it.'

'Yes, but what about tea-time?'

However, it turns out to be unhideable, and as soon as Pauline sees the wound, Mama is told and James is terribly scolded, and I am rushed into the car and then from the local infirmary all the way to Edinburgh for an emergency operation that very night, to extract the bullet that is travelling behind my eye.

'It is scarring the tissue on the back of the eyeball,' says the man in a mask who has threaded a needle to keep my eye open, so the white lights can glare inside and leave stains on my vision that I cannot blink away.

It is all quite exciting until the moment I awake, with a banging in my head, and my face has heated up so I think I will explode, and water is pouring around my eyes and I fall back into a terrible dream of milk-white figures through a film, and hear a stranger's voice calling from a far-off place, 'There now, the pain will be better soon.'

I come back from hospital with a hole between my nose and my eye, and a round white patch to wear over it. I am proud of it as a war wound until James won't catch my eye, and no one seems to be talking to him much, and I see it is because of me, and I am filled with longing for us to be friends. But I am sleeping downstairs in Mama and Papa's bedroom, all those stairs and corridors away from the night nursery, until my eye is healed and I don't have to wear the white patch any more, so James will play his own games with Hugh, and not look at me at all.

Though I like the smell of wax in my parents' bedroom, there are different ghosts here and I don't know where they will creep from, but tonight I am cosy by the fire and the sitting room is only next door. Papa has lit the fire and I can watch the flames dance on the ceiling and that will keep the prickly swooping feelings from fingering me out of the blackness. And when the fire goes out it will be time for their bed-time and then I will be safe with Papa there to breathe his warm breath in the dark.

But I want Papa. I lie in bed trying not to want Papa, watching the flames, hearing their gentle crackle. There is a sheepskin rug next to the bed. My parents' four-poster bed is opposite, and the shadows flicker inside it. I want

Papa. I could go next door into the light of the sitting room but I am scared of Mama's eye. But I want Papa, I want him to hold me in his big arms.

I step out of bed and feel the sheepskin rug on my feet, soft under my toes. I look into the fire and find the warmth to travel the darkness round the other side of the screen through the door and the dark alcove, to the sitting room.

The door squeaks open. I slowly put my head round. There is a silence in the room. All is still. Mama is not in here, just Papa sitting in the blue armchair. I am so relieved I scamper round the sofa and between the armchairs to sit on his knee. But there is something strange in his eyes. I stand before him, and look up at him. He looks at me almost as if I am not there, and then looks back to some faraway distance as if his eyes are on elastic.

'Papa,' I say, 'Papa!'

Again he brings his eyes back and looks into mine with a terrifying intensity. I am looking into a black chasm. It is so sudden I dart back in shock.

Suddenly I hear Mama's step outside the door, she is carrying a tray, I can hear the clinking. I rush to hide behind the log basket, it is near the door to the bedroom, maybe I can escape without being noticed by her.

She comes in. I crouch down. She is bringing in their supper. She stands before Papa and puts the tray on the newspaper table in front of him.

'Don't tell me you haven't been drinking!' she hisses.

'I'm sorry, darling,' says Papa sadly. 'I'm sorry, so sorry.'

I creep through the door and back into their bedroom. I sit on the bed knowing there is a secret I cannot grasp, knowing from the atmosphere, knowing from the faraway look. A cold wind blew into my face from the chasm in his eyes.

The fire burns down to a glowing ember. I feel the white cotton patch over my eye is wet, the wound has broken, and my head is cracking, a worse pain by far than when the bullet entered.

I want James to talk to but he is all the way away in the night nursery, and won't even look me in the eye. I want to curl up in Kitty's bed but she is staying with the cousins.

I feel cold, the fire is going out but I dread them coming back to bed in that gloomy four poster creeping with shadows. I get into the bed made up on the sofa, in between the cold sheets.

I fall asleep and when I sleep I dream of the night sky. I reach up my hand to touch it and find I am touching the face of the night. I polish the face with my hand and it begins to shine gold. I look into the eyes and they look into mine with a long simple look as clear as stars. It seems to fill me with a sweet light. I wake with tears in my eyes and the sunlight shining through my lashes makes hundreds of tiny rainbows that I examine closely, magenta, orange, lime green, electric blue, I want to see all the colours.

'Well, I think our little soldier is ready to get up now!' says a voice from behind the colours.

'All right, darling!'

The voice is standing on the other side of the room, folding something.

'All right, darling?' she repeats.

'Yes,' I say in a small squeaky voice, trying to place her.

Mama comes over and stands at the end of the sofa.

'I think it's time for you to go back up to the nursery now, don't you?'

I nod.

'Darling, you have been so brave.'

I sit up and smile at her. Something from inside me reaches to her.

But her body stiffens and she backs away from the bed.

'Come now, up you get, you can get dressed upstairs.'

I collect my clothes, put on my slippers and make my way upstairs to the nursery.

In the nursery they are having breakfast. Doreen gets up and takes my pile of clothes from me. The coal fire is lit. Pauline looks nervously at Doreen as she ties Annie's bib.

James is sitting over his porridge and does not look up as I enter.

'Have you got your pads?'

I have them in a plastic bag. She shakes her head. 'It hasn't even healed yet,' she says to herself more than to me and changes the pad over my eye.

'Well, your *brother* has been perfectly happy without you!'

I look down.

James looks nonchalantly ahead of him chewing his porridge.

We walk on either side of the creaking pram in a glum silence. The air is cold and clear and I can see all the way to the dovecot at the end of the avenue. A mist hangs above the grass in the distance, I can see my breath. There are patches of snow still lying. We walk along the road to Mrs McCready's house, the birds sing in the clear air.

Doreen seems oppressed by our silence. She sighs.

'Go on, you two, go off and play!'

The freedom is unusual and we run away as fast as we can in case she changes her mind.

We run through the white gate, down the Station Road, and clamber into the back woods before we slow down.

'She wouldn't even be able to find us now if she wanted to,' says James.

'No! We're safe as houses,' I say.

'Safe as trousers!'

'Safe as mouses!'

'Let's go rolling,' says James.

We find a good spot and roll all the way down through last autumn's leaves.

'Look! There's snowdrops!' Tiny shoots beginning, lots of them in a hidden warm place under the trees, the pussy willow has tipped the ends of the naked branches with silver paws.

We walk through the wood as soldiers for a while, getting away from the cold as usual, and climb on to the old railway track where the dark-orange bracken grows high and we can't see over. We have to tread carefully along the side of the track in case it is mined but James has a 'photographic memory' and has seen the enemy plans so he knows exactly where to tread and I have to follow in his footsteps.

I get tired of this and suggest that maybe overflying planes might spot us from the air, and better 'take cover', so we take cover and navigate the barbed wire back into the woods where the growth is thick and we have to beat our way through with sticks. When we reach the top of an incline we are startled by the strangled sound in a tangled leafless bush. A great black crow is flapping or trying to flap, stuck in the bush's tangles. We stand watching it in horror.

'You're a horrible crow,' shouts James unexpectedly.

'I hate you!' I scream too.

'You're evil!' says James. 'You peck out lambs' eyes!'

I am frightened of its black eye.

'You're evil,' I say.

'I hate you!' screams James again. 'Let's kill it!'

He picks up a stick and pokes the crow, I pick up a stick and poke the crow. James thrusts the stick into the struggling cawing crow's open mouth, I thrust my stick in too. Yellow stuff comes out.

We do not know if we have killed it but we run. Run through the brambles, run through the bracken, run down the hill, run along the grassy ridge of the old railway track until we are breathless.

But we cannot outrun the pathetic sight of the wounded crow, trapped but alive, with some yellow juice of death coming from its beak.

'Well, it pecks out lambs' eyes.'

'Yes, we rid the place of it.'

'It could probably peck out a lamb's eye and eat its brain even.'

'But it wasn't dead when we left it.'

'It nearly was though.'

'Probably it was dying anyway trapped in that bush.'

'Yes, we put it out of its misery.'

'Yes, it would have died anyway, only slower.'

'But it wasn't dead when we left it, was it?'

We look at each other.

'No.'

We wander along the track until we come to the gate. We climb over and into the green grass under the tall beeches.

'We could make h.q. here,' James suggests.

We pile up some sticks and make h.q. We sit down on the sticks.

The air is getting damp and droplets of water glisten on the grass. The sky is bright white through the naked branches above us.

In h.q. you make plans.

'Could follow the burn round,' says James. We can hear it rushing from here, big with meltwater.

'Not enough time before tea,' I say.

'Sorry about your eye, Speck.'

I shrug.

'Hospital was OK.'

'Well, we could go up by the ha-ha and through the cherry orchard.'

So we leave h.q. and set off for the cherry orchard.

We wade through the waist-high grass among the cherry trees and feel the silver-grey curling lichen on the shiny bark. Our legs are getting wet.

'Why did she let us go, anyway?' I ask.

'Oh she's going on holiday soon, so she can't be bothered.'

'Who will look after us?' I am hopeful that nobody will. James shrugs.

'I think she's called Carol.'

My heart sinks.

I'm on the front lawn, the grass is wet. I am frightened. I get down under the rhododendron branches to hide in the old Tree House. Carol is calling from the nursery window, and I feel cold. Her voice is cold, her breath smells of iron. I can smell the earth, the wet rhododendron leaves have turned yellow and black. She has red veins in her eyes, the whites are yellow. I don't want to be in this cold place. I run up the bank through the long wet grass to find the yew tree. The trunk is green and powdery. The poisonous red berries fall among the needles, and white juice comes out when you squash them.

I crouch beside its wide girth, in the dark-green shadows, whispering made-up songs with my hands over my ears.

The snowdrops die in the moat and give way to gold and purple crocuses. Something is beginning to quiver in the gnarled fingers of the old cherry trees. It makes the air gentle.

The blue-green folded-up leaves of daffodils poke through the wet grass in multitudes by the stretched-out paws of the stone lions at the top of the drive, and through the dark sodden leaves that lie under the tall beech trees.

'You're dawdling,' says James.

'I know,' I say.

'Well, come on then, or she won't let us out on our own again.'

'Can we run away?'

'Yes, OK, we can run away tomorrow.'

'No, now. Can we run away now?'

'No.'

'Why not?'

'Everyone knows that you have to plan an escape!'

Carol is sitting on the fireguard, her stockinged feet stretched out in front of her, smoking a cigarette. She has red crinkly hair and rough pock-marked skin. She has large hands. The smell of her feet mingles with the cigarette smoke.

'Where do you think you've been?'

We mumble.

'Sit down!'

We sit down.

The table is set up in the corner while Mama and Papa are away.

Carol has finished feeding the baby. She has buttered me toast and Marmite, but the taste burns my mouth and I don't like it.

'Eat up,' she says.

'I don't like Marmite,' I whisper.

'I said eat up!'

She has a metal smell. She puts her face close to mine and the smell comes out of her mouth.

'Eat up, you little baby!'

I try eating the Marmite.

'I said NOW,' she says.

I can't get the toast in my mouth in time. She thrusts my plate away and tears the piece of toast out my mouth, she lifts me up with a jerk from my chair and forces me roughly into Annie's pale-blue shiny high chair, pulls the straps out from underneath my legs and ties me in tightly, then yanks my legs down under the tray.

'There now! That is the place for babies! Babies go in high chairs. How do you feel now, like a big baby? You look like one! Just a big baby!'

I look down at the tray trying not to breathe.

'Well?' she says. 'Babies have to drink out of babies' cups!' She gets up to fetch Annie's cup from the pantry.

I look at the tray. I feel ashamed, I can't look at James. I feel a tear collecting behind my glasses. I lift my eyes and catch James glinting at me.

'Now, Corporal, chin up! These Japs are well known for their cruel methods of torture. For King and Country! We'll be out of here soon, I'll recommend promotion. You say, "Yes, sir." '

'Yes, sir!' I say, my lip still quivering.

'That's right,' James whispers. 'I'm making plans for the you-know-what!' He winks at me. I begin to breathe again.

Carol returns with the plastic mug with the beak and places it on the tray of the high chair.

'Now, James, watch your little baby sister, she can't even sit at the table yet, she has to drink out of a baby's mug, not like you, you're a big boy, look, James.'

James turns to her with a serious expression and with dignity salutes and says, 'YES, SIR!' loudly.

Carol is taken aback, and I start to laugh, and I can't stop, then James starts to laugh until we are both convulsed in helpless giggles. Carol bangs the mug down and shouts, 'James, go to the bathroom and get the potty!'

James goes to the bathroom, and Carol yanks me out of the high chair and my legs get caught, she pulls until one of my sandals slips off and I slide out. James brings in the potty and puts it down in front of the fireguard and stamps his foot and salutes. Carol makes me take down my trousers and sits me on the potty.

'Little babies have to do a wee after tea,' she says.

But the spell has been broken, James has left the room

58

and is marching up and down the nursery corridor shouting, 'Achtung! Achtung!' and I can't go so Carol loses interest. She lets me get up even without going and I run to join him.

I wake up in the night and the room is pitch black, I can't see in front of my eyes. I need to go to the loo. Doreen leaves the door open and the light on in the corridor, but Carol has closed the door and there is no light shining through the crack. But I need the loo. I must go, I pull back the covers and sit on the bed. I feel the shiny eiderdown under my fingers. My feet dip into the darkness. My hands stretch out before me as I try to feel my way towards the door, across the wide-open plain of the night-nursery floor. My heart is beating, I can see flashing colours in front of my eyes. I am trying not to panic, I reach out and out, my toe catches a mysterious edge, I feel disoriented. Why is that there? I thought that was in the other direction, if that's the fireguard . . . I reach out my hands to alter my direction, rising panic, breathing more quickly, I bump into a metal knob. That must be Hugh's bed then, if I follow it round I'll reach the wardrobe. I can follow that to the door. But it turns out not to be the wardrobe. I need the loo badly now, and I can't find the door, or even the edge of the room. Then I feel the shiny wood under my feet, I have come up against the wall. But which wall? I know I can't hold it in much longer. My toe touches James's cowboy hat, I can feel the fringes. I will go in that, it is dark, no one will notice it. I lift up my nightie and piss in the hat, I feel the water running under my heel, it comes in a gush. I try to get away from it in the darkness. I have no idea where I am in the room and I don't know how to get back to my bed, I begin to cry and I feel the tear running down my cheek. I am whimpering when I hear a little noise.

'Inny, inny.' It is Hugh's voice feeling its way into the darkness. I follow it until I come to the side of his bed.

'Inny,' he coos, 'inny wenny snow.'

'Yes,' I whisper to him, 'I'm lost.'

'Nena wenny inny.'

'Yes,' I say, and climb into his bed.

'Deedy inny nena.'

'Yes,' I say. His warm little body is all curled up and cosy. I curl up beside him and hold him till I am asleep.

It is when I am having breakfast, sitting up on the shiny white chair that Carol comes in with a glaring look. James looks from her to me. I am trembling, she is marching towards me with such a strong force. She grasps my wrist and pulls me off my chair, I am pulled along behind her trying to find my feet, her pace is relentless. She drags me through the door of the night nursery and I catch the side of my face on the door, I put my free hand up to my face, she jerks the other and points to the cowboy hat and beside it, a puddle of pee.

'WHAT is that?' she says pointing her large hand.

I look up at her, unable to speak.

'What's wrong with you now, CAT got your tongue? Has it?' She bends down and her metal breath comes into my open mouth. I try to frame the words but no sound comes out.

'STAY RIGHT THERE and don't move!' she orders, and returns with a bucket and a cloth. She pushes them into my chest.

'YOU clean it up! You are disgusting, do you hear me?' Her mouth with its metal smell comes up to my face again. 'Do you hear me, YOUNG LADY? You are disgusting! I've never met such a disgusting child as you. Now tell me what you are! Tell me!' She pushes my shoulder. 'Tell me!'

I say in a whisper, 'I am disgusting.'

'Say it louder!'

'I am disgusting,' I say and tears are pouring down my face.

'Now clear it up!'

Thankfully she leaves the room, and I get down on my knees to chase the puddle of wee across the slippy surface of the shiny wooden floor.

James saunters in. I am still trying to wipe it all up into the bucket. He looks over me.

'Oh Specky, did you do a piss in my cowboy hat?' He lifts it up and smells it. 'Oh yuck, Speck, I can't wear it now! Never mind,' he laughs, 'I'll give it to Tommy.'

He smiles at me and nudges me, but I am all ashamed and a tear crawls down my cheek.

'Come on, Speck.' He gives me a gentle shake. 'I don't care about the silly hat. I'm not surprised you thought it was a loo, it looks just like one!' He laughs again.

I know he is trying to cheer me up, but I just cry more.

Suddenly I blurt out, 'She says I'm disgusting, she made me say it.'

'Ooooh!' says James as if he knew all along, 'that is a torture technique. They stick bamboo shoots under your nails and light them, then they do brainwashing. In the prisoner-of-war camps it's a bad business.'

He is an expert, he reads the *Tyger*, and sometimes the *Eagle* and I can't because there's too much writing and I get bored. I read *Twinkle Twinkle* which is about a little girl with big eyes who puts her teddy to bed.

'Is this in the story?'

'Oh yes! Forcing you to even drink your own wee!'

I agree with him that that would be worse.

'Anyway, Major, I have thought seriously about offering you up for promotion, even recommending you for the VC.'

Everyone has arrived. The hall stairs are thronging with people. There are uncles with long legs and small smart children. The air smells of pot-pourri. We go in a troop through the green glass-paned door and along the black passage to the servant's hall while the uncles hide the eggs. There are rosebuds opening on the wall and long benches to run around.

'It's time.'

We run in a screaming crowd along the black passage to the chapel door and squeeze out into the herb garden to find the eggs which are hidden everywhere around the Garden.

Clementina has a large canvas bag to make sure she can collect as many as she can see. Most of us put them in our rolled-over jersey or make little piles by the balustrade. The lawn glints with metallic magenta, green and gold. Tiny eggs have been strewn across the grass. The sun lights up the colours. I am fascinated by Clementina as she hurriedly climbs trees, scrambles into bushes, jumps down steps and thrusts other smaller children aside to make sure her bag is fuller than anyone else's. She does not even like chocolate, she just wants to win.

'I know where one is,' says a tall, kind uncle who leans down and whispers to me.

I smile up at him and see him looking at my small clutch.

I look at it myself and look at him again. I put my hand in his and walk with him across the lawn to a tall beech tree at the edge.

'No helping!' shouts Clementina from across the lawn. 'The hiders can't help the finders, it's not allowed!'

'I didn't hide it,' winks my uncle, 'I just saw it and I'm not going to show you where it is.'

We stand at the bottom of the curling rhododendron and the flickering light through the leaves makes me sleepy. I see a multi-coloured Smartie egg in the top branches. The tall uncle smiles and pushes me towards it, then ambles slowly across the lawn.

I climb up and wrest it from the branches and watch through the shiny leaves all the children scurrying across the lawn in excitement. I lie along the branch like a snake and slowly unwrap the chocolate from pink metal paper. I suck the egg so the chocolate melts and through the leaves watch Clementina as she stealthily edges around the balustrade, looks from side to side and quickly scoops all Tommy's eggs into her bag. She hurries off, stops, comes back and leaves three or four small eggs in the place where the pile had been.

I am holding my breath. It is not good to see these things.

Clementina races across the lawn to the fountain where James is wading through the spray to collect an egg deftly placed on the shoulder of the man who blows his horn of water into the air. James is getting sprinkled with the spray and a small crowd of adults and children are watching. When he retrieves the egg he lifts it in the air and the sound of their clapping echoes against the house.

I look across to see little Tommy approaching his pile of eggs in dismay. I see him kneel down and look up and around, baffled and bewildered. No one is about. He stands up, opens his mouth and wails. Jean, his nannie, rushes from the side of the balustrade where she is talking with Carol, to see what has happened. All he can do is point at the eggs and cry. I watch Clementina by the fountain look nonchalantly across at the noise and straight back to the fountain. A few people look across from the fountain to the wailing Tommy who cannot be quieted and is beginning to stamp his feet, unable to communicate his loss. Jean begins to smack his hand vigorously which makes him wail louder but with a different kind of pain.

I slither down from the branch, I hate what I know. I am frightened of Clementina. I run across the lawn over the bouncing grass.

Children and grown-ups gather beneath the music-room windows, Tommy still whimpers. James has a glow of triumph on his face. He is jumping about, I tug him by the sleeve. He turns to me.

'Hiya, Speckled Eggy!' he says and laughs at his joke. I look round for Clementina.

'What,' he says, 'what is it?'

I put my hand up to his ear and whisper through his dark curls.

'She took Tommy's eggs.'

'Who did?' he says aloud.

'SHSHSH!' I say. There is chatter around us, but Clementina can always hear her own name.

'Clementina,' I whisper.

James looks at Tommy.

'Oh, is that why he's bawling his head off?'

I nod.

'Oh for crying out loud!' he says and puts his hands on his hips. 'Well, let's sort that out then.'

He is in his Captain Scarlet mood. Clementina is talking to a grown-up cousin, dangling her bag behind her leg and kicking it. I watch with my mouth open as James steals a handful of eggs from the gaping bag, and looking at me with a gleeful twinkle, succeeds in gently prising out a large green egg in a cardboard box. He turns around and hides this in his jumper, and walks towards me with a swagger, and a bulging stomach. Tommy still quivers with departed sobs, next to his diminished pile of eggs. James carefully places the eggs in the pile, then pulls out the one from his jersey and exclaims, 'Look! I've laid an egg!' Tommy smiles at the joke, and gazes silently at the eggs. James ambles over.

'I'm a hero!' he says, and beats his chest with his fist. 'Call me King Egg, you're Speckled Egg. OK, Speggy?' He laughs again.

We are standing on the bank in the sun. It is time to roll the eggs. My eyes are closed and the sun shines on to my eyelids. Through the laughing voices I can hear the woodpecker drilling holes.

Large baskets are filled with brightly painted eggs. Jesus left the tomb empty and the boulder rolled all the way down the hill. We painted the eggs all colours in the kitchen with our aprons on. Mrs McCloud lifted them out of the huge silver saucepan, and let the steam rise off them till they were cold.

Everyone is being handed out an egg.

I choose one from my aunt's basket. It is turquoise with a white moon. I don't want to roll it down the hill to see whose rolls furthest and see it smashed at the bottom, but that is the way it's done.

We are lined up in a long row. All the children and the grown-ups. One of the uncles leaps down and holds his hand up to stop everyone throwing their eggs and says we must pose for a huge long photograph. We have to hold our eggs up. I am standing between two small cousins.

Then we count down loudly to the moment. Five, four, three, two, one, and suddenly all the eggs are hurled into the air and down the bank, very few are rolled. I hurl mine too and I watch it rolling and skipping across the tufts of grass and reeds to rest at the bottom.

Uncles leap down the hill with their long legs to judge who has won. They reach the bottom and begin to argue. Papa also runs down the hill and before long, James and Clementina and some older cousins have joined in. One uncle throws an egg at the other as he walks away. It smashes on his head. He turns round, picks up an egg, smashes it in his hand and rubs it in Uncle Finnie's face. Papa roars with laughter and picks up an egg himself and throws it at Uncle Bill.

I am trying to see where my egg has got to through the legs and people and decide I had better try to rescue it. By the time I reach the bottom of the hill to find my turquoise egg with a white moon pieces of egg yolk and shell are flying through the air and uncles are in tangles rolling down the hill shoving bits of egg into each other's mouths, faces, down necks, up noses, over clothes.

My egg has come to rest in a reed clump and I scramble between the legs and arms and shouts, and clamber up the hill feeling my hair where bits of egg are stuck to it. Jean and Carol are standing with their arms folded looking furious and disgusted. The aunts and Mama are looking a little perplexed and all the smaller children, who have been forbidden to join in, are jumping up and down on the bank. The tangled battle scene seems little from high above, with missiles flying out of it. All at once it winds down and they are walking away from each other and climbing up the bank with their shirt-tails hanging out and egg yolk and bits of shell sticking to their hair, and laughing and punching each other.

I look at the crowd on the bank and in a horrible moment catch Carol's eye looking at me, as though it was my egg that started the fight. I hide it in my jersey to keep it safe.

James comes up before me and smiles. His hair at the front is sticking straight up and egg is smeared down the side of his face.

'Look, Specky.' He shows me his sock that has had egg crammed into it. 'Uncle Bill did that!' He empties it out.

Carol and Jean look on in a silent fury, unable to vent it when so many grown-ups were involved. I watch the stragglers lift themselves on to the road.

I bring my blue egg out from my jersey.

'Look! I kept it safe.'

'What for?' says James.

'I don't know.'

*   *   *

I tiptoe across the evening-damp grass. I have sneaked out of the music-room door, down the steps and across the lawn. I am very awake. I carry my turquoise egg. The birds are beginning to call their evening songs. Cuckoo spit wets my legs and cobwebs have been woven between the low twigs. They pull strands across my face. I walk with excited unknown purpose through the naked saplings and into the darkening wood. The air is still. Faces stare from the leaves. They look straight at me.

I make my way to the old yew tree and stand before it.

'This is a moon egg,' I whisper, holding up my egg.

The quivering tree stretches above me and spreads its branches down around. I kneel down and hold the egg on my lap.

I dig a hole among the needles and between two large roots, and further down into the damp earth, digging with my fingers till my nails are full of dirt.

I lift the egg up to the tree silently and then place it in the earth. The people are listening. I blink three times to tell them I know they are there.

'You are safe now. You will be safe here.'

I cover the egg with earth and needles, get up and brush myself off. I walk slowly through the wood, then run full pelt across the grass and back through the music-room door. The gloaming turns blue in the yellow light.

Carol is leaving. Mr Chisolm puts her bag in the boot. She is sitting in the front seat looking ahead.

'She's going to be put on trial!' James whispers as the car door slams.

'Is she?'

Mr Chisolm starts up the engine.

'Yes, it will last for a month.'

'Then what will happen?'

James looks at me with the you-mean-you-don't-know look.

'They'll chop her head off!'

I gasp and quickly look back at her sitting in the car, her head still there on her shoulders.

'Does she know?'

James slits his eyes and shakes his head slowly.

'Not yet.'

With mixed feelings I watch the car drive away.

When it has rounded the corner I notice that hundreds of daffodils have opened.

We run across the gravel between the stone lions and down the drive across the grass, through the sweet clear air of evening sunlight.

We climb over the gate covered with frills of silver

lichen and up the avenue, and begin to walk so that we
don't frighten the ewes with their new lambs. They get
down on their knees and pull at the teats, while their tails
wriggle quickly.

The crows are calling up in the beech trees that line the
avenue.

Mr McCready is standing far off whistling to the dogs.
He stands leaning on his tall crook. We watch him telling
the dogs what to do in the language he shares with them.

'Giddon, girl, giddon,' says James briskly as we amble
towards the shepherd.

'Oh shut up!' I say and refuse to become a sheep dog.

Mr McCready puts his cap on the back of his head and
winks at us. He has sky-blue eyes. When he looks at me I
feel the sky inside me.

'Ay, grand day, grand day,' he says without really
opening his mouth.

We sit and watch with him for a while, watch the dogs,
watch the sheep, watch the sky and the day passing and
the few lazy insects murmuring among the tall grass.
There are spit bugs that stick to the stalks in their frothy
homes.

'Race you!' says James, jumping up and running.

We run through the line of beeches into the meadow
and climb across the barbed-wire fence into the wood.

The wood is damp and cool and we walk between tall

ferns. Entering in among the trees the ferns are less dense and sorrel and celandine are growing. We crouch down to pick the delicate flowers with lilac veins and eat them, they are tangy. Violets grow in the hidden corners under mossy stumps.

The air is filled with birdsong, hooeet and chicha chicha, and trrrrrip dip, eeeet, whistling and pips and short trills and long melodies. We stand listening and the breeze in the new leaves makes the shadows dance among the ferns.

'Right, you stay there and I'll do the ambush.'

'No! I don't want to play soldiers!'

'Go on!'

'No! Let's play orphans running away.'

'That's sissy!'

'Please.'

'No, you be the Gerry.'

'NO!' I stamp my foot and sit down on the log and realise it is wet but I have to stay there getting wet. James stands there and sighs.

'You're in a bad mood, you don't even want to be a dog today!' This he finds hilariously funny and starts to laugh. I sit there getting crosser and my bum getting wetter.

'Shut up! I don't want to play any game with you!'

But James just says, 'Woof!' and starts laughing again until he can't talk.

'Aw come on, Specky! Don't get in a huff, we can play spies. Let's be in enemy territory, then take the information back to headquarters. You can even be the top spy.'

I sigh.

'What do spies do?'

'Oh, they just go along.'

'All right then.'

I get up and sadly feel my bum. We climb down the hill to the burn. The water glows orange in the sunlight, and the stippled brown trout dart to safety when our shadows hit the water. We walk along the side of the water watching for the green-brown shadows. We take off our socks and shoes and wade across the slimy stones, grasping the exposed roots that ripple with sunlit water shadows. The air smells of nettles.

I hear giggling from behind me and look round. James's shoulders are quivering but he raises his eyebrows and pretends to look innocent.

'What?'

'Why are you laughing? Shut up! Why are you laughing?'

He can't contain it and bursts into full laughter.

'Your bum! Your bum! You were sitting there with that face on and all the time your bum was getting soaked. Oh I can't help it, Specky, honestly, I just can't help it.'

'Hmmph!' I say, struggling with the infection of his laughter.

'Well, so what! Shut up!'

We pass a herd of forget-me-nots glowing from among the nettles and dipping their faces into the water, and behind them, up in the wood, a yellow crowd of buttercups.

The stones are sometimes sharp, and the water is deep in places.

'Hey, wet pants, d'you want a rest?'

'You SAID I was the TOP spy!' I turn round and shout and in turning fall down in the water, and sit stunned and frowning with the cold water flowing round me.

'OK, top spy wet-trousers,' says James, holding out his hand to help me up. 'On your feet, Sergeant, we don't want you catching a chill.'

'Bugger,' I say.

James pats me on the back.

'Spoken like a true soldier.'

'Are you my shadow?'

I am sitting on the hot pipes in the bathroom and out of the window I can see the tops of the trees swaying slightly in the wind.

'I said are you my shadow?'

I am puzzled by the question.

'No.'

'Then what are you doing sitting there?'

Doreen is standing with her hands on her hips.

'Waiting for you to come out the loo.'

I am on the top pipe almost at her eye-level.

'And why are you waiting?'

'I don't know,' I say quietly. 'I don't know why.'

'Listen,' she says more kindly, 'you can't follow me round all day, holding on to my skirt, laddering my tights. What's got into you?'

I hang my head down and look at the black lino, and the green legs of the bath.

'I don't know,' I say more quietly.

But I do know, I just can't say. I am frightened she will go. That if I let her out of my sight for one second she might go on holiday again and I would walk into the nursery to find Carol holding her own severed head.

I look up at Doreen, she has a locket round her neck. Her Bill gave her that.

'Don't go,' I whisper to the locket.

'I'm not going anywhere yet,' she says in her loud voice, but her big hand reaches across to touch my hair. 'My oh my, there's a bird's nest in that hair I'll have to see to after lunch. Now run along downstairs and help with the flowers, Mama wants you at eleven. There now!'

I jump down from the hot pipes, and follow her up the nursery corridor.

*　　*　　*

There is a secret staircase in the music room. It leads up behind the organ. We have been up there, struggling through the cobwebs up the tiny ladder to that magical place where many thin silver flutes stand in rows, from the very thinnest reedy piccolo to the deep vast echoing sounds of the tuba. It is a forbidden place. It is right inside the organ. We can pick the thin flutes out of their wooden stands and blow through them, and we can look through the grille and the wooden cherubs holding garlands into the vast music room below and see the six tall windows on two sides reflected in the shining wooden floor.

Mr Chisolm is a man of few words. He is thin and wiry with white hair. He fought in the War, James says, and that's why his ears are frostbitten. Often, sitting behind him in the car when he is dressed up in his chauffeur's cap, I examine the strange nibbles that have been bitten out of his ears.

His workshop is between the gun room that smells of gun oil and the locked passage to the sacristy that leads to the mysterious silence of the chapel. It is behind the room that has a secret staircase to the hidden door in the music room.

Mr Chisolm and Stuart brought trestle tables into the saloon and set them up in front of the windows that look down the front drive. The door on to the balcony was open this morning, birdsong and wood pigeons from the damp and misty air called into the house from the avenue, calling out of the mist.

Then Callum brought white and red lilies from the Greenhouse and Mama spread an enormous drugget over the saloon carpet. She brought many vases to arrange the flowers in. Clementina, Kitty and I sit on the drugget with her, helping to arrange them.

Mama places a white wire ball in the bottom of the large vases to stick the stalks in. The secateurs snip the ends of the long stalks, and cut the leaves from the stems.

I cannot make the secateurs work and my stalk gets chewed in their sharp blades. The juice comes out on my fingers and smells bitter.

'My stalk won't cut,' I say, showing it to Kitty.

She takes it from me and gives it a perfect snip.

Mrs McCready and Mrs McKay are unfolding a white linen cloth over the long trestle tables. They work silently.

'Mine is the best!' says Clementina, sitting back on her heels to admire her arrangement.

'There's no best,' says Mama, 'they're all lovely!'

My vase so far has one flower in it.

'Kitty can help you with yours, Elizabeth.'

I look at the red threads and yellow stamen inside the lily.

'Now, Clementina, you can start a new vase.'

Clementina sighs.

'I don't want to much.'

James comes tearing through the double doors of the saloon, stops by us, falls down on his back and sticks his feet straight up in the air, then plonks them down with a bang and lies there without moving.

'What are you doing?' I lean over and whisper to him.

'I'm dead!' he breathes.

'Do you want to help me put flowers in my vase?'

'No, yuk, that's for girls,' he says sitting up on his elbow. 'I'm helping with the chairs.'

'I'll carry the chairs too,' says Clementina, standing up.

'Who asked you?' says James.

'I can do it better than you can!'

'No you can't, you're a GIRL.'

'Oh shutup, you're just a twit anyway!'

'Darlings, do stop it. Clementina, go and help the men carry the chairs if you want to.'

Clementina strides out the room, without looking at James.

He shrugs and puts his hands up. 'Silly old fart!'

'James!' says Mama.

Mrs McKay and Mrs McCready are bringing trays of polished wine glasses from the pantry and arranging them in rows on the white table-cloth.

I stick another lily into my arrangement. Mama picks

up two large finished vases and clinks through the saloon doors and downstairs to the hall.

'Come and see in the music room!' says James.

We run past the sitting room and along the music-room passage filled with light from the garden through the row of tall arched windows that reaches the floor.

In the music room the chairs have been set in rows facing the organ. Some are still stacked up.

A man with a great shock of grey hair is standing beside the grand piano talking to a small woman dressed in lilac.

'Marvellous acoustics!' he is saying and his voice echoes across the room. The organ stretches its tall flutes up to the ceiling behind his head.

Other chairs have been arranged in two crescents facing the others and violin- and trumpet-shaped black cases lie strewn around a crowd of music stands. The small woman seems to be washing her hands together and looks up at the grey-haired man, smiling and nodding, and washes her hands some more.

Stuart and Mr Chisolm are carrying chairs through the music-room door, up the stone stairs from the chapel passage.

I run back to Kitty, she is clearing away the stalks. All the vases have been filled up. She looks up and smiles.

*   *   *

'Now you two remember and behave. Sit quietly and don't get in anyone's way.'

Doreen is giving my hair a final brush through.

It is after tea and I am dressed up in a pink smock dress and white cardigan.

James is wearing his kilt and red flashes to keep his socks up. He is jigging about.

'I'm going to get up next to the conductor and do the Highland fling!' says James and bursts out laughing.

'You'll do no such thing, young man!'

'Yeah we will! Won't we, Specky?'

He does a twirl with one hand in the air above his head.

'Will they sing?' I ask.

'No, just play their instruments. Now take them down-stairs.'

Kitty is dressed up too, in her blue dress with the large white collar. She takes us both by the hand.

James skips along the corridor and pulls Kitty's hand up and down. We look through the banisters and see people collecting downstairs. They are dressed in long dresses and black suits. Many people are walking up the stairs from the hall.

We can feel the evening wind coming all the way from the open front door and filling the house with the smell of lavender, cloves and rose petals. There is murmuring and chattering, and the slippy sound of long dresses as they walk along the landing.

James leaps down the stairs, two at a time, and jumps seven on to the landing outside the sitting room.

The music room smells of lilies. Everyone is taking up their places in rows, and the musicians are opening their cases and arranging the music. The fire is roaring up the chimney, stoked high with wood, and some ladies are shifting their chairs away from it.

We are directed by Papa to sit on the square green sofa at the edge of the room. When the room is naked of chairs and the wide shining floor a vast empty space we take the cushions off the sofa and run full pelt across the floor, drop the cushion and slide through the sunbeams across the shining wood.

The musicians begin to tune up.

Miss Dougall has been invited. She is sitting at the back in a peach suit and matching hat. She wears the peach skirt sometimes for lessons in the schoolroom with a lacy shirt and her pearls. She teaches me four-times table, and b-a-t, b-a-l-l, b-r-o-o-m. I watch her mouth when she says the letters. Her face is covered in powder. It sticks to the hairs on her top lip. I watch the hairs when her lips move to see if it falls off, but it just sticks there.

A hush falls, and the grey-haired man takes up a position with his hand in mid-air.

He lowers his hand and music begins. Little and trembling at first, it seems to rise up into the ceiling and fade into the circle of white roses. Another strain rises and seems to tangle up among the festoons that the wooden cherubs are holding along the wooden rim of the ceiling.

Suddenly a tumult of sounds fills me up, and sends me into a trance, then slips me out of it, and I go tearing into a wide-open starlit sky. Violins suddenly rub me and roll me between their coloured strings and purple and gold flutes send me spinning and bouncing back on to the floor. I lie there breathing very quickly until a great surge tumbles me back upwards and little flowers seem to open and blossom inside my hands. An indigo light picks me up and soothes me and I fly back into a violet sky. The huge room is breathing coloured sound. Suddenly an oboe begins to haunt me and I want to run away into a far distance except the violins catch me up and I am spinning and bouncing again between their coloured strings.

The music fades and ceases. Everyone begins to clap. We clap the music away until it has completely disappeared.

'Are you enjoying the concert?' asks the tall woman I am being introduced to. I shake her hand and curtsy.

'I don't know,' I mumble.

Mama looks at me and turns to the lady apologetically. 'She's in a world of her own.'

'Well, it's difficult for them to appreciate Mozart at that age,' says the lady kindly.

I go to look for James among the forest of legs and hands holding glasses of wine and oblong yellow cheese on sticks, and find him sitting cross-legged under the white tablecloth.

'Hiya, Specky Wecky Decky Lecky.'

'Hiya,' I say and sit down beside him.

'James?'

'Yep!'

'Are you enjoying the concert?'

'Bloody boring! Where's the beat?' He pouts his lips and plays imaginary drums. 'Did I tell you I'm gonna be a drummer?'

Then he looks at me with a serious face.

'Slob de doolly wolloby flobberlake, tooddellee wollop?'

'Proberly wobberly,' I answer, and we both giggle.

After the interval the room has grown dark except for the musicians' end. Outside the night has fallen, and candles are lit on the windowsills.

A flute begins to play alone. I am glad that by the fireplace someone has opened the window. The silver thread leaves through the crack for the small people in the garden to listen to under the leaves. It is an aching song. I hear them listening with their eyes open and feel them whistling with the blue wind. And in the vast room filled with a single silver flute and flickering with fire and candlelight I feel their presence entering and encouraging us to slip through the secret door the music is opening into that other world.

Dark-green ferns brush my face, and I'm in a forest by a blue lake. A note with terrible longing makes a flower open in my chest till I can hardly breathe, and into it flies a little gold bird with a long beak that sings a sad song. The flower opens more petals and sings a gentle song back that comforts the bird a little. For a while the flower and the bird sing a song together until the moon calls from the distance and the bird flies away to it.

The music begins to light up unusual colours in the air, and I see people have flowers on their heads. Some are open and others are closed.

I travel through a tunnel of dark-green ferns, and smell the smell of hedges. Papa is carrying me along the corridor by the Egg, I can see the tops of the pillars through half-closed eyes. I am carried to a rhythm. Within me musical patterns and coloured shapes are humming and changing places. I don't want to leave this world and I keep my eyes closed as I am handed over to

Doreen, changed into my nightie, and folded into cool sheets.

'There now, off ye go,' says Doreen patting my behind. I follow Mrs McKay's and Mrs McCready's bustling over-alls down the corridor.

Mrs McKay's pantry is full of brushes, mops, polish, dusters, brown paper and a basket of shoe polish with brushes and rags. I have been equipped with a yellow duster, a pale-blue dustpan and a small brush with red stripes on the handle.

'Now, Morag,' says Mrs McCready, 'I think we'll get the job done in no time, wi' the help we've got.'

'Ay, so we will. We're lucky, aren't we, Rina, tae have a grand worker helpin' us along.'

Mrs McCready turns round to give me a little wink.

'Whit a shame we dinne get such a treat every day.'

'Ay, we'll just have to make the most o' it, Rina.'

We travel from the green bathroom to the yellow bathroom to the flag room dusting and hoovering and polishing and out into the long corridor at the top of the stairs. There is a tall window at the very end that reaches to the floor. I can see the copper beech. It shimmers in the wind.

We go into the fountain room with its cascading bed-stead.

They make the bed together and unfold the crisp linen sheets.

'Och, it's bright ootside today.'

I climb up on to the window seat and see the fountain in the garden glint in the sun.

We bustle from one room to another.

I dust the yellow brass light switches, and sweep with my dust-pan and brush under the frills of armchairs, double beds and sofas. I polish the orange shiny wood around the edges of the carpets, and the white wainscoting. I caress the paws of sofas and the twirling legs of tables. I follow the curling plasterwork and dust the little white eggs. I polish in between the tall legs of the great glass case that holds the disintegrating flag that was carried at the battle where men fought with gold swords in a flooded field. And then, among the black foliage of the banisters, I greet the little gold birds.

'Yer doin' a grand job!' says Mrs McCready.

'Ay, we'll have to tell Doreen tae give ye two biscuits at elevenses.'

'Oh, I'm fair lookin' forward tae ma break, Morag!'

'Ay but no' yet, Rina! We'll can get the queen's room finished and that'll be us.'

We walk along the dark corridor and around the Egg.

There is a heavy black four-poster bed of thick ebony and deeply carved in the queen's room, and on cither side of the bed is a cabinet with a glass case above it. One is filled with magnificent coloured butterflies, purple, magenta and lemon yellow. The other with green metallic beetles, large hairy spiders and blue insects.

Mrs McCready makes faces of disgust as she spreads out the sheets while trying not to look at the spiders.

'Och, disgusting beasts!' She shakes her head quickly. 'Ah dinne like this room at a', ah dinne ken how folk . . .' She looks at me and stops. I am dusting the pearly iridescent dishes on the desk. They change from pale green to violet.

We shut the door when it looks neat. The queen's room is a dark and heavy room, but glitters with treasure if you can stand the death.

In the nursery the radio is playing. Pauline reaches to turn it off when I follow Mrs McCready and Mrs McKay through the door.

'No, dinne,' says Doreen, 'that's the Tony Blackburn show.'

Tony Blackburn says, 'And for all you lovely ladies, here's Johnny Cash.'

'Ay, that's us!' says Mrs McCready smiling.

Everyone takes their place at the round table, and I have Ribena.

Mrs McKay sits down and musters herself up.

'Well now, have you heard?'

Doreen glances towards me with a warning look at Mrs McKay.

'It's nought the bairn canny hear,' she says half aloud.

'Well, what is it then?'

'Jim McCloud!'

'Whit aboot him?'

'Well, has he no' been invited tae the big lunch!'

'How?'

'He's in wi' they friends of Sir John's brother, up at Whitelaw, yon folk that gang aboot in the caravans.'

'Hippies, they're ca'd.'

'Ay, whatever. Any road, they're comin' tae the big lunch. Well, that's fine, ah dinne mind, wi a' they bangles and coloured clothes like, ah dinny mind, I'm open-minded like. But ah draw the line at Jim McCloud, ah'm sorry but ah dae.'

'How? Has he been invited like?'

'So ah heard.'

'Well, Morag, it's nought tae do wi' you, hen.'

'Well, ah'll no serve the likes o' him!'

'Och, he's no a bad lad.'

'Rina! wi' that long hair and a' that!'

'Ay, but he's a nice enough lad.'

'Well, it isne right fer the likes o' him to be sittin' doon tae lunch at the big hoose! It isne right, and ah'm no servin the likes o' him!'

'Ye canny gan past him wi' the dish, ye ken.'

'Ay ah can! It's a downright disgrace! He canny sit doon wi' the Lady, it's no his place!'

Mrs McCready sighs and places her cup down.

'Ah canny abide folk thit are above their station,' continues Mrs McKay, 'and ye ken what that means,' she says pressing her chin into her neck and giving Doreen a knowing look.

I am sitting on the edge of my seat watching from one face to another without moving my head, just my eyes behind my glasses. I can see Doreen's look as she closes her eyes and nods.

The two of them like to talk about the 'airs and graces' of Mrs Fergus.

Mrs McCready makes an attempt to change the subject.

'Now did ye see *Coronation Street*?'

But Doreen ignores her.

'Ay well, Morag, ah ken whit yer sayin', like.'

'Ay, well, there ye are. Its a' the same thing.'

'Airs and graces' are lipstick that is too pink 'for a woman her age', boots with a heel, and 'carrying on in front of the Lady' as if she was one of 'them'. I imagine them also as gold lace piping, and a floating coloured wind with stories in it.

Mrs McCready sighs and turns to the quiet Pauline.

'And how's yer mither keepin', hen?'

90

'Fine, thank you.'

'And are ye goin' home tae see her soon?'

'Ay,' says Pauline.

'How's her leg these days?'

'Och its no sae bad as it was, ken, she's doin' away.'

I look into the bottom of my cup and my Ribena has finished. I get down from my seat and climb up on the toy box and look down on to the garden and far away to the blue hills and see that the top of the tall wellingtonia is swaying in the wind.

The night nursery is lit by the yellow side light. There are long shadows in the folds of the green curtains, and a deep shadow in the corner beside the tall mahogany wardrobe and the medicine cupboard. I keep my eye on that shadow.

'Stop looking there,' says Kitty. 'No one lives there, it is a good place.'

I look at her to see if she really means it. She has the light behind her head and the wispy hairs around her face are lit up. She is sitting on top of the eiderdown while I am snuggled down inside the bed.

'James says "He" lives there!'

'Well, I met him, and he was very nice.' Her face is in darkness but her eyes shine with their own light.

'Oh.'

'Anyway, he isn't there very often, mostly he lives outside in the garden.'

Bumhug crawls down from behind Kitty's hair and scuttles across the eiderdown, sniffing the air with quivering whiskers. I lift up the sheet and watch his long pink tail disappear under the covers, and feel the claws on his feet walk down my body. He reaches my feet and I feel his fur brushing my soles.

Kitty is opening the book and finding the page.

When Bumhug and Candida first arrived they lived in the newspaper room next to the hot room where warm pipes filled the air with heat. They had many babies together until their cage was too small and Kitty let them run freely.

I never really knew if it was James who left the door open so they ran along the black passage in long lines, and sent Mrs McCloud into a frenzy, so Stuart had to come and collect them all into cardboard boxes. But when Mama heard how many there were she put on her driving gloves and sat with her hands on the steering wheel looking straight ahead until Kitty climbed in the car with three cardboard boxes and forty-two rats, to drive to the pet shop in Edinburgh.

'Are you listening?'

Kitty has her arm around me. I am lying with my head on her chest and can feel her voice vibrate within her.

I nod.

Bumhug crawls up my other leg.

Kitty begins to tell the story and I fall into a dream. I am standing in the garden. The air is turning blue. Under my feet the grass is damp. I bend down to sniff the earth. I follow a path, barefoot into the trees. In the deeper shadows, clusters of perriwinkles glow violet, and the tender melodies of pale-pink-breasted long-tailed tits, still gathering moss and cobwebs, echo among the leaves.

There is someone there in that dark corner, under the yew, someone fragrant with forest scent, playing fluty sounds on a whistle. I stand in that place listening to the stories it plays, seeing patterns among the darkening twigs.

And woven in and out are the threads of another story, about a walled garden filled with delicious fruit, aromatic herbs and sweet lettuce. Kitty's voice is soft and constant. A broken-hearted husband longs to steal the lettuce for his beloved wife, and scales the wall and jumps into the garden.

Then suddenly it is Kitty who has scaled the walls of the kitchen garden by the climbing tree and is snaking under the blackcurrant bushes so the clusters of shining fruit brush her hair. She jumps across the path and slithers under the strawberry net and lies still. She listens for Mr McKay.

Her eye is looking right into a strawberry plant where she can see a little pale-green fruit with a red tinge and yellow pips, hiding in the middle.

She can hear the keeper's dogs barking far away in the distance. Slowly, she begins to gather fruit for her own beloved.

'Who is he?' I interrupt. 'What does he look like?'

Kitty does not say his name, she tells me other things, and I see him riding a horse across the night-nursery ceiling.

From far away up the garden by the blue-blossoming artichokes comes the terrible sound of Mr McKay's Wellington boots, striding along the soft sandy path. CHUGGED CHUGGED. Kitty hears him and holds her breath. Her heart beats faster as the sound approaches, slowly, steadily nearer. Her heart stops when he halts in front of her.

'GET OUT FROM UNDER MY NETS!' he roars.

Like a newt in a fishing net she squirms and wriggles free. She stands up straight before him with straw in her hair, clutching the squashed fruit in her T-shirt stained red with strawberry juice.

'Lights out!' says Doreen, opening the night-nursery door and poking her head round. 'It's time that Elizabeth was asleep.'

'Oh but she's just been caught!' I say.

'No buts, I said. Lights out now!'

Kitty nods.

Doreen leaves.

'Oh, but don't leave her there, what will happen?'

'It's all right, she gets free in the end, and she lives happily ever after.'

'But does she give the strawberries to . . .'

'Don't tell.' Kitty whispers quickly.

'Don't tell what?'

She closes the book and kisses my cheek.

'You know, about what I just said.'

Bumhug returns to his home under her hair.

I shake my head. 'No, never!'

When the light is turned out I lie in the darkness and watch the stories weave themselves together in the crack of light, so I can remember all that I must never tell, and in the shadow next to the medicine cupboard a tall man sits on a black-and-white horse.

I walk into the kitchen holding Doreen's hand.

'Have ye a minute for a cuppa then?' says Mrs Fergus.

'Ay surely,' says Doreen, 'that wid be fine.'

We sit down around the square red table that looks out on to the back yard. Mrs Cowe has two yellow fingers, she lights a cigarette between them.

'Mary,' she shouts, 'we're sat doon if ye want a cup!'

Mrs McCloud is in the scullery. I get down and run through to see her behind a hill of potatoes.

'Tea's ready,' I say.

'Ay hen, ah'll be through in a minute.'

She beckons me over to look at the gnarled face of an old potato, it has a big nose and two eyes. She makes it say hello to me.

I reach up and kiss him on the cheek and the grit gets on my lips. I wipe it on my sleeve.

'Did he like that?'

She puts the potato up to her ear and opens her eyes wide.

'Och ay! He's right chuffed.' I smile. The potato plunges into the pool with the others.

'And here's Callum comin' the now.'

I climb up on the chair and between the sinks and see Callum walking up the yard with a box of fruit. He walks in the back door and past the cold larder, where meat sits under net pyramids to keep the flies away.

He places the box full of punnets of strawberries, blackcurrants and raspberries on the scullery table.

'That's fer yer Summer Pudding, Mary.'

'Ay, grand.'

'Mary!' shouts Mrs Fergus from the kitchen. 'Mary, will ye just come through and hear this!'

Mrs McCloud and Callum exchange a look which seems to have understood all the Mrs Ferguses of the world.

'Ay, I'll be through shortly.'

'Ah'll bring the lettuce up this afternin,' says Callum.

I run through into the kitchen to understand the commotion.

Mrs Fergus has a look of bright indignation on her face, she is shaking her head.

'Och, that'll right, is it? Mrs hoity toity thinks as she's too good tae serve at table! Honestly, can ye just see her sayin' it!' She looks at Mrs Cowe.

'So it's got to be a duke now for her tae hand roond the spinach! Ye ken whit a'm sayin'? Just who dis she think she is like! Mary are ye hearin' this?'

She turns to Mrs Cowe again. 'No good enough for her, like. Who is *she* like?'

Mrs Cowe nods and puffs at her cigarette.

'Mary, are ye listenin'. Yer Jim's no guid enough fer Mrs McKay!'

I look carefully at Doreen who is shaking her head too.

'Ay, she said it wis a disgrace that the likes o' him should sit doon at table wi' the Lady.'

'Likes o' him. LIKES O' HIM! Mary, will ye come through now and listen to this!' And whispers, 'That lad, ye ken, that lad is the apple o' Mary's eye! Nothin' is too good fer him, ye ken, nothin at a'!'

Doreen nods. 'Well, she's some high ideas sometimes.' She raises her eyes to upstairs. 'She's got some fine ideas aboot hersel'.'

'Well ay, yer tellin' me!'

'Whae dis she think she is like?' Mrs Cowe enters the conversation.

Mrs McCloud sways slightly from side to side as she walks and the flowers on her apron light up in the sun.

'Mary, de ye hear this? Now sit doon, here's yer tea.'

Mrs McCloud looks surprised by this unusual attention. She sits down.

'Now then,' begins Mrs Fergus, 'now then, Mrs McKay says as yer Jim has been invited tae the big lunch, bein' as how he's friendly wi' Sir John's brother's friends. Now then.' Mrs Fergus takes a breath, she is beside herself. 'Now then, Mrs McKay says she willne serve him at the table! She said she'd just ignore him, like, as if he didne exist, she willne, any road, she willne serve him!' At this she crosses her arms over her chest and looks at Mrs McCloud with pursed lips.

Mrs McCloud slowly sips her tea.

'Ay well,' is her response.

Mrs Fergus is not satisfied.

'She said he wisne guid enough!'

'Ay well,' responds Mrs McCloud.

Mrs Fergus says loudly and slowly, 'Morag McKay says

that yer Jim isne guid enough fer the likes o' her!' she says, pursing her lips again.

'Och aye,' says Mrs McCloud, sipping her tea again.

'He'll be sittin' up there at the table and that old besom will walk past and ignore him just as if he wisne there!'

Mrs McCloud puts down her teacup.

'No she willne.'

'Ay she will!' Mrs Fergus beams.

'No she willne.'

'Ah'm tellin ye, ay she will!'

'She willne.' Mrs McCloud shakes her head. 'Because ma Jim widne sit doon at the table upstairs if ye paid him, he widne feel comfortable. Ah ken ma lad.'

Mrs Fergus looks defeated and turns to Doreen. 'Some folk willne be telt!' and shakes her head.

The door by the chapel is open into the herb garden Bushes of rosemary and thyme and mint mingle the air with interesting scent.

The peacock is strutting by the flowerbed, his long tail flowing behind him like a gown. He is pecking the heads off the pinks. He does not eat them and their heads lie uselessly severed on the grey stone slabs. As we walk around the beds he lifts his head back and opens his beak to call his loud plaintive call. I see the sound ripple up his turquoise throat.

'Shut up!' says James who does not like the peacock.

'Shut up, stuck-up!' he shouts again.

We climb up the steps and on to the lawn and run across to the fountain. The spray ripples the water in a gentle sound. We lie down in the grass by the moss-covered rim and look into the world of stringy algae and crowds of tadpoles. In the pile of stones at the centre where the stone man sits blowing his pipe of water spray live the orange-bellied newts.

James is rolling up his trousers and Kitty is hitching up her skirt and they are wading in amongst the darting tadpoles to try and catch them in handfuls. But the sky is so vast and the smell of azaleas so strong and the sound of the spray and the bees buzzing among the flowers so gentle that I lie on my back and look into the blue and enter into another place.

'NO! James, NO!'

'Go on, I dare you, you do it!'

'How can you!'

'Like this!' and I see James swallow a tadpole.

'Go on, I dare you!'

Kitty looks down at her cupped hand. 'No, I can't.'

I am concerned for the welfare of the swallowed tadpole, but some little feeling is calling me from the faraway trees and I get up and slowly wander across the soft grass, away from the gazing house, out of the sunlight and into the quiet shade.

There is a smell of wild garlic here, growing from the exposed damp earth. I walk over the green mossy stones, and bend down to pick some wild hyacinth glowing blue violet from the shadows. Under the beech tree my bare feet touch the curly husks from last year's autumn. I bend to collect a few, and put them in my T-shirt. I find the tail feather of a hen pheasant, striped brown and black, and a snail shell with a yellow spiral. I put it to my eye to see inside.

I sit on the dark-green log, staining my knees as I climb on to it, to survey my gathered treasures in a shaft of sunlight that is carrying the breezy leaves and makes the ground seem like underwater. I climb down when I am satisfied and make my way through the bendy ash saplings that hit you in the face if you are not polite and very slowly slowly make your way round and in between them. I have been watching all the way till now the green shoots push their way out when the buds open their four small doors. Now they display their frondy leaves and stroke my face as I walk past.

I know my way. I watch my legs be touched and tangled by the shadows of the breezy leaves that are fluttering in the sunlight in the tree tops.

Through the ferns, now, to the wilder part of the wood, no one comes here much, and gently, silently the atmosphere changes as I enter the world of the singing people.

They sing silently and I have to stop and be very still in order to hear them singing. They too are shy and I have to give them time to have a look at me. I feel it when the air suddenly throngs and I know I have been invited in, as their dancing presences pass through me as shafts of sunlight pass through my eyes.

I make my way to the tall green yew that spreads its branches around it like a house. I know which side I must enter through, then walk backwards all the way round the tree and enter in the other way. That is manners. It is dark inside the tree's branching arms, a dark green light, that smells sweet and strong. I feel the singing people watching but they know very well that the gifts I have brought are for them. I arrange my offerings with care in the shelves of the old yew, and think they look nice in the holes. I decorate the holes with the tips of fern fronds, and sing a short song that has no words. I can hear them listening.

That is enough now, and it is time to leave. I walk backwards out of the yew tree, turn around three times, and return to the lawn the other way, through the old dogs' graveyard, where Tippet and Motrum and Badger are buried. The moss grows over the stones. Some of them died even before Papa was born. Through the beech trees and out into the sunlight again.

I run across the lawn. Kitty is kneeling down making

daisy chains. I ask her to show me and she makes a slit in the stem.

James is trying to lift into the air the blue-and-red kite that Uncle Patrick gave him last Christmas.

'Come on, wind!' he shouts, 'blow a bit, can't you? Bloomin' heck!'

From the house's huge face one of the eyes in the top right-hand corner opens and a head pokes out, then a hand, and we hear the sound of the nursery bell travelling through the air, and a small far-away up-above voice say, 'It's tea-time, children.'

The tea table is pulled out in the middle of the room and the grown-ups from downstairs are already sitting down to tea. Papa, Mama, Father Crane and a pallid guest with glasses. She is sitting next to Clementina, who is 'making conversation' with her. Clementina is good at 'making conversation', all the grown-ups do it at dinner and it helps things go smoothly. Annie is in the high chair being fed by Pauline and Hugh's eyes are just about level with the yellow-and-blue tablecloth. There is toast to eat, and sandwiches and fruit cake and cake iced by Mrs Fergus, and scones, malt loaf and Selkirk bannock.

We sit down.

'. . . because it's a special day,' Mama is saying, 'Father,' and she smiles kindly at Father, 'is going to say Mass

tonight for us. So if you could have them ready for seven.'
She turns to Doreen, with a slight smile and raising her
eyebrows, 'That would be lovely.'

'I hate bloody God,' James whispers to me.

I am so shocked that I start laughing and of course
James starts too so then we are both quivering with
giggles.

'Up your bum, God!' says James quietly, and I am
completely helpless, with tears streaming down my face in
uncontrollable mirth.

Mama looks at Doreen who looks at us and says, 'Now
quieten down, you two, you're at the tea table!'

But we can't, so we have to be separated and put at
either side of the table and not look too much at each
other.

I look instead at Father Crane's nose. It sticks out so far
it has a corner in it, and inside the nostrils is black shining
hair. I notice the same hair sprouts out of his ears and, as
he is bald, I wonder if his hair grows on the inside instead
and comes out the holes. I heard Mama say that he speaks
through his nose, so I am watching it to see if I can catch it
speaking.

I notice James is also watching his nose and wonder if
he is trying to as well. The weight of our eyes on his nose
seems to make it twitch and suddenly an enormous hoot
comes out of it into a handkerchief.

'Oh please excuse me, Lady Mary!' He turns to Mama apologetically.

'Not at all, Father, not at all.' She smiles to one side with a forgiving look, and then moves her mouth back into an ever so slightly disgusted expression. But he seems satisfied that he has been forgiven.

When we get down, I hold Papa's hand along the dark corridor and feel blissfully safe. He has huge tender hands and mine is completely enveloped. I march past the portrait of the white-haired man in a glow of safety.

'Why were you looking at Father Crane's nose, Lizzie?'

'How do you know I was looking at it?'

'Because I saw you, how else?'

I reach my eyes up towards his. We come out into the light of the stair landing. He stops and looks down at me with his head on one side, waiting and smiling.

'Do noses ever speak?' I enquire.

He starts to laugh, a deep vibrant laugh, I see a tear at the side of his eye, he too cries when he laughs. He does not answer my question though, he just reaches down and picks me up, and tosses me on to his shoulders so my legs are around his head, and I am high, high in the air, with a magnificent view. He holds my legs and I hold his forehead, and we go lolloping down the stairs.

*   *   *

There is a crescent moon in the sky and darkness over the garden. An owl calls from the hills beyond.

'This will be your room soon,' says Kitty from behind the curtain. I jump off the toy box and through the curtains.

'Why will it?' I blink in the yellow light.

'I'm going to boarding school and you and James are moving out of the night nursery.'

'I'm going to boarding school too!' says James.

'Yes, but you're still moving in here with Specky. It will be your bedroom in the holidays.'

'Are you going away like Clementina goes?'

'Yes.'

'And is James?'

'Yes.'

'Will I go?'

'Not yet. Girls don't go till they're older.'

'I'm older than Specky!' says James, from the carpet where he is lying with his legs straight up in the air.

'Yes, we know that.'

'But will I go when I'm as big as you?'

'Yes. You can have my bed when I go,' says Kitty.

I bring the chair up close to the bed and climb up on to the slippy purple eiderdown to be next to her. She is leaning her head over and sewing a name tag on her blue socks.

I like the idea of being inside Kitty's big bed.

'Will it be nice at boarding school?'

'I don't know,' says Kitty.

'Will James like it?'

'He might, he will play cricket.'

'Over!' shouts James, kneeling up on one leg and hurling his arm round and round.

'Will you play cricket?'

'No, it's a boy's game and my school is for girls.'

Clementina's empty bed is on the other side of the room.

'Which one does Clementina go to?'

'A girl's one, of course.'

'When she grows up will she still be a girl?'

James is preparing to climb on to the wardrobe.

'James, don't do that, get down!'

'Just one quick jump!' says James.

'Don't! You'll get me in trouble.'

'Just one quick jump!' says James, and climbs up on to the walnut wardrobe and hurls himself on to Clementina's bed.

'James, that's enough!'

'Just one more jump!' says James, sliding off the eider-down.

'If Doreen comes in she won't let you in here again.'

'When Specky and I sleep in this bedroom, I'm going to do that every night as part of my night training.'

I sigh.

'Do what you like, but not while it's my bedroom.'

Then a terrible thought strikes me.

'Who will sleep there when James has gone away?' I ask, not wanting to hear the answer.

'No one. Like now, when Clementina is away no one sleeps there.'

'So will I sleep in here on my own?'

'Yes!' says James slithering himself into Clementina's eiderdown, 'and the white lady will creep along the corridor and haunt you at night.' He pulls the eiderdown over his head.

'Wooooo!' He walks around the room, being a shiny purple ghost.

'Don't!' says Kitty. 'You'll frighten her.'

'Waaaaah!' says James.

'Is it true that the white lady comes?' I turn to Kitty.

'No!' says Kitty.

'Just because you've never seen her,' James wails, 'doesn't mean that Specky won't.'

Doreen opens the door suddenly, comes into the room and pulls the eiderdown from James's head.

'Just what d'you think you're doing? Can't you be left alone for a minute without causing havoc?'

She lifts the eiderdown off him and the hair on the top of his head stands up straight and follows it.

'Oh I'll be glad to get you off to school, young man!' she says, spreading it back on the bed.

I am far from sure now. Perhaps army training all through the night would be better than an empty bed and the corridor with greenish light waiting for the white lady to come. I slip off the bed and back through the crack in the curtains, to look at the moon casting shadows in the garden.

The chapel is cold. The cushions dig zigzags into my knees. Father Crane drones on in Latin. The rain patters against the window, and I watch the shadows trickle down the straw matting. Mama turns the thin gold-edged page of her missal and clears her throat. She is following. And I am hoping that she doesn't know. The lilies fill the air with scent. Papa is sitting with his face in his hands. It is a long Mass. I dare not catch James's eye, he is serving on the altar and rings the silver bell. Father Crane wears green and gold. Like Cinderella he has many splendid frocks. There is a fly caught in the window crack which buzzes with a frenzy. The long ancient words. I am hoping that Mama doesn't know.

Because we found our way through the door that is always locked, and walked up the silent corridor that is cold and bare.

The door of the sacristy creaked open. The room had an alarming stillness. The priest's clothes had been carefully spread out on the cabinet, green with a gold cross in the middle. His white cassock hung on a peg. There were flowers on the windowsill and the room smelt fresh.

'Let's go,' I said, catching Our Lady's eye and feeling Mama's presence in the room.

'Don't be silly, we're here now.'

We knelt down and opened the drawer to find the rice-paper wafers wrapped in white tissue, and the large shiny ones with an imprint of Jesus being crucified.

We had five each and one big one. James broke the bread in half and said in a solemn voice, 'This is the body of Christ.'

He opened the altar wine and poured out a capful. We drank it in turn. The sweet sherry trickled down our throats. James poured out another, and drank it, and then put the bottle to his lips and took a swig. He replaced the cap.

We began to see things in a delirious light. We took the cassock from the peg and both got in it together.

'Let's be a church ghost!' said James when we were inside the cassock.

'What does a church ghost say?'

'It says AAAAAAAAAhhhhhhmmmmeeeeeen!' he wailed and I joined in and then we got the giggles because we couldn't get the cassock off and we rolled around on the floor in a tangle, and I can see the traces of dust on the hem of the cassock, and I look at Mama to see if she sees too.

We tried to put everything back straight but nothing seemed to fit together through that strange sweet blur.

But Father Crane has turned round and is holding up his hands.

'In nomine patris, filii, et spiritus sancti.'

'Amen.'

We stand up. His dirty cassock returns to the sacristy. James and I look at each other and his eyes twinkle. I look at Mama but she is closing her missal and folding her mantilla. She doesn't know, perhaps she doesn't know.

We genuflect and race from the chapel along the dark corridor and up the front stairs, through the saloon, under the Egg and into the dining room for breakfast. Wednesday is the day when we have dining-room breakfast and we sit on the big chairs with curling handles and drink tea out of white porcelain teacups. It is the day when Papa lifts us up on to the tall marble fireplace to sit on the mantelpiece so we can observe the long room from a great height and see the blue hills far away through the windows. I can see as far as my great-great-grandmother can, whose portrait I must not lean back against. It is too far to jump. I have to call to Papa, 'Will you get me down now?' and he pulls back his chair, strides across the room and stretches up with his great long arms and I slither off the marble slab that makes my bottom cold.

Father Crane lives in the flat above the scullery. James and I have sneaked up there to look. It had the same chill silence as the sacristy. The bed was made, his slippers neatly together under the chair. The air was musty. A bare room except for the crucifix and the missal. It chilled my blood and I wanted to get away right away.

James agreed so we ran down the green stairs and back into the scullery.

He does his work in the book-lined library. It means getting out all the gold-edged books and spreading them about to look things up and take notes. Papa said, 'PLEASE can you tell him not to put them on the billiard table!' and Mama breathed a sigh inwards and nodded with her lips together. Maybe taking notes from gold books is not so important as billiards, but Mama didn't think so.

Sometimes we play Frieda on the billiard table after dining-room breakfast. Racing round to catch the white ball before the pink ball stops. Today we play James's game, Army Training. Sliding across the wooden shelf, jumping on to the long green leather sofa with worn-out arms, up on to the coffee table, and the chair with a red seat, the desk, and mind the blotting paper, then slide along the hearth, across the logs in the log basket, and up on to the shelf careful of the music box playing 'Three little maids from school are we,' all without touching the floor.

The tall door opens and everyone stops. I'm in the log basket under the slidy shelf, James is on the long green sofa, Kitty is up on the coffee table and Clementina is on the hearth. Father Crane walks in. 'Ahem,' he says, which he always says, because really he is a bit nervous of us and would prefer to be looking things up and writing them down.

The bottle-green sofa smells of leather, the room smells of old books and wood. We sit in a row on the sofa. Bits of lichen from the log basket are sticking to my socks. Father Crane sits opposite on a straight-backed black leather chair with studs.

'Now what do you think Jesus meant when he said that some seeds fell on hard ground and some seeds fell on rock and some fell on fertile soil?'

'He meant get Callum to point you out a good patch to make a garden in,' says James.

'Ahem, I don't think that is quite relevant.'

'He meant he's not a very good gardener!'

'Now, no need to be facetious.'

'He meant . . .'

Kitty nudges James.

'It would be better if you thought a little before you spoke,' says Father Crane.

Clementina sighs loudly.

'Elizabeth, do you have any idea?'

I shake my head.

'Kitty?'

'I think he means that some people can't understand things, and some people won't hear, and some people will understand and make something of what he's telling them.'

'That makes me the rock and Specky the hard soil then!' says James, pulling a face.

'Not at all!' says Father Crane, 'it reveals that you have understood perfectly.'

James screws his lips to one side.

I don't understand anything at all. I just try and see Callum in the garden but turned into Jesus with ribbons of blood flowing from his hands while he plants seeds and throws them about carelessly, not the way Callum does, each tenderly placed in the earth, as though he's putting them to bed.

'So a parable is a story that has a message.'

'Will ye no ferget ma messages,' says Mrs McCloud to her son Jim.

Her messages when he returns are a roll of sausages, a loaf of white sliced bread and half a pound of butter.

'Now, Elizabeth, do you understand what a parable is?'

'It's a story with messages in it,' I say.

'Well done! Can you tell me a message from a parable?'

I look at him and get caught up in his expectant face. I so want to give him a good answer, but I cannot tell him about the sausages.

'Do they come from the butcher?' I say hopefully.

James creases up with laughter.

Father Crane looks puzzled and disguises a sigh.

I notice Kitty's lips held tightly together to stop laughing.

'Don't throw pearls before swine,' says Clementina drily. 'That is a message from a parable and it means don't expect pigs to understand wisdom.'

James is quivering with giggles and tears are pouring down his face.

'Well, pigs go to butchers,' says James through his tears.

And as I know that sausages come from pigs I am satisfied that I have caught the general gist.

'Ahem, well let's go back to the Commandments that we were talking about last week. Clementina, can you give us a Commandment?'

'Oh yeah, she can do that all right!' murmurs James.

'Thou shalt not kill!' says Clementina through her teeth while looking at James.

'Thou shalt not kick and bite and be a dirty fighter!' interrupts James.

'Ahem. Thank you, James, but Clementina is telling us.'

'Well, she does, there should be a Commandment against it!' James says under his breath.

'Now, Elizabeth . . .'

'There's a Geneva Convention, I don't see why there shouldn't be a . . .'

'Yes, James, thank you. Elizabeth, can you tell me about the Commandment, Thou shalt not steal?'

I am suddenly terrorised by the altar wine, spilling into the cap and on to the black lino of the sacristy.

'I've never stolen anything!' I say, panic-stricken.

'No, no, it's all right, I'm not suggesting you did.'

'I didn't even know about it.'

James nudges me. 'Be quiet.'

I turn to him. 'But I've never been in there before.'

'Just STOP talking, OK, Specky?'

I turn to Father Crane, with my mouth shut.

'Ahem, yes,' he says. 'Very well. Er, Kitty, would you like to read us the prayer on page eighty-two.'

Opposite the forest of blackcurrant bushes, the sweet peas grow up a trellis outside the potting shed.

It is a hot, still day. The sky is blue and the bees are buzzing among the flowers and fruit. Mama is at the sweet peas with her secateurs. She places them in the low wooden basket, she has on her gardening gloves and a pale sweet pea pink-and-white scarf around her neck. Her hair is up in a bun and a brown curl escapes down her neck. Snip Snip.

James is skipping up and down the path in his shorts and sandshoes, his knees are covered in mud.

I am helping Mama put the flowers all straight in the basket so the coloured ends face the same way. I like helping her. I want her to tell me that they look nice and I have done it all right.

'Darling, do pull your socks up! Look, you have left one out.'

I feel untidy and awkward.

'Come on, Sergeant, let's go on a training mission.'

James takes one jump over the hedge and lands on a discarded flower. I look up to Mama for praise for my arrangement but she is reaching up among the flowers. I run down the path with James, past the strawberries ripening under the nets, past the tall artichokes that have bloomed purple like giant thistles, between the tall yew hedges and down the Lady's Walk. The grass path runs between flowerbeds filled with red-hot pokers and dahlias, gladioli and huge crimson daisies with black-and-yellow middles. Mr McKay's honey bees live and buzz in this heady atmosphere of colour and scent and this is the very path that Beauty walks up and down so forlornly with her paintbox, waiting for the Beast. Kitty has read me the story on the nursery sofa from the Ladybird book. The Beast, in his blue satin suit with the lace collar, was sad too. But I never minded the idea of marrying a gorilla. When he turns into a Prince his face is pale pink, his hair is bright yellow, and I don't like his haircut.

We sit at the end of the path in a seat with curling handles, under the weeping willow that weeps over the square stone pond covered in moss and filled with water lilies.

'OK, we need a plan,' says James.

'What plan?' I say and sigh. I prefer to make it up as I go along.

'Well, we could ambush Callum and raid the potting shed for supplies, then we could take the supplies back to the men that are stationed behind the lines, I know they're short on rations. Are you ready for your orders, Sergeant?'

'Aye aye, sir.'

'No, Specky, you have to say, "Yes, sir," we're not on a ship, you know!'

'Yes, sir.'

'And salute, you have to salute.'

'Yes, sir,' I say, and salute.

'Very good, Sergeant. Now, keep a close tail on me and keep down.'

So we run along the side of the peas, squatting down, and snake our way on our bellies past the carrots, and past the frilly cabbages, and dodge behind the pear trees, whispering and ducking, until we reach the door of the greenhouse.

We can see Callum in among the rows and rows of carnations, through their blue-green stalks. He is knobbly like a tree, with a square head and huge hands covered in earth. He wears a leather waistcoat. He has a mystery. He knows the secrets of roots and bulbs and blossoms, and if he is not one of 'them', he is at least half. His Wellington boots are the size of Papa's but the rest of his body is small, and I am sure that at night he joins them under the moon, hundreds of them beating rhythm with their feet and exchanging the hidden stories.

They say he has green fingers and as I see they are not green, I take this to mean that sometimes they sprout green leaves. I am in awe of him. 'We dare not go a-hunting for fear of little men.' And I know that though Mr McKay is the king of the greenhouse and the kitchen gardens it is Callum who makes the flowers grow.

'Get down or he'll spot us.'

I am perfectly aware that though Callum has not looked our way, he knows we are there. He moves away into the potting shed and we quietly open the door into the hot damp greenhouse full of smells, sweet and prickling layers of them. The nettle tang of new ripe tomatoes, the thick sweet smell of figs, the light fragrance of the carnations, mingling with the dripping damp stony places under the tables where little white and purple flowers grow wild.

We crouch amongst them as Callum's boots enter the room and walk up and down between the aisles. There is a tank of water with a hose-pipe in it, the surface ripples as he walks back and forth.

He leaves again and we scuttle round the corner into the room filled with fleshy-leaved potted plants, and tall Arum lilies with thickly powdered yellow stamens that comes off on your nose when you smell them.

When we hear him go out to the covered beds at the front, we run into the potting shed. There is one low window, and the sunlight streaming through it lights up the swirling dust beams. It smells of earth. The shelves and the surfaces where Callum does potting are red with it. There are rows of earthenware pots in all range of sizes, and long bunches of raffia hanging from the rafters. There are tools and spades and trowels and forks for sewing and growing and hoeing and planting and tending. Different jars hold different thicknesses of wire. We steal some lengths of wire for making horses and some raffia to wrap around our wire people and we dart out of the potting shed when we hear his footsteps.

'Is that enough supplies?' I whisper to James as we stand in a white corner next to a vertical pipe.

'No, we need food supplies.'

'We can't steal anything from in there, though, Mr McKay . . .'

Mr McKay has a red face that goes redder, he has a boiling inside him that sometimes boils over, he is ferocious, and no one steals fruit from his greenhouse.

'Yes, we can easily, don't be a scaredy, I can easily climb up the fig trellis.'

'No, James. No, James, please don't.'

I can't bear that he is so reckless and unfrightened.

'But anyway, it's against the Commandments.'

'Raiding isn't the same as stealing, didn't you know that!'

'Don't, please.'

'Why not? It's easy!'

And I know that I have made it more likely by wanting him not to.

'But what if Mr McKay comes?' I can't help saying.

James shrugs nonchalantly.

'He won't!'

I follow James down the bright corridor to the end house, pulling on his sleeve.

'Please don't, James, we're not allowed.'

'Everyone can do exactly what they want! "Not allowed" is for grown-ups.'

He opens the door into the rich scents of the fig house,

and the room is dark with the leaves that grow in profusion up the walls and across the roof.

'I can get up and pull one off, what you so scared of?'

He climbs up on the slatted shelf and like a terrible dream I see Mr McKay's bald head approaching from a distance between the carrots and the leeks.

'James, it's him! It's him! Get down!'

'Oh Specky, I'll not fall for that one.'

'James! James!' The panic is rising inside me. 'I'm not lying, I promise. Look! He's coming, he's coming right now.'

Then we hear the door open at the front and his self-assured step walking through the carnations and along the passage.

James turns to me, his face is white. He stands frozen on the shelf afraid to move. I see him listening with his eyes and holding his breath. Mr McKay has stopped.

'What is he doing?' James crouches down on the shelf and we wait and listen. Through the glass I see him coming this way. Just then Callum passes him with a box of plants. He puts down the plants and holds him in conversation. Mr McKay looks cross. I can't hear their words. Mr McKay stomps off the other way and nods something at Callum.

When he has turned the corner into the potting shed, Callum silently and swiftly opens the door to the fig house, motions us to get down and through the door and hurries us out the front past the carnations, pressing three tight red tomatoes into my hand as he closes the door. We run down the path and through the buttercups next to the bee hives, and don't stop running until we are out of sight of the greenhouses and free to breathe.

We are lying on the grass at the front of the house. Far away down the drive and up the avenue I can hear the sheep bleating and the high-pitched whistle of Mr McCready as he talks to his dogs. A sky lark is dipping above and singing a crazy song. Down in the grass with the beetles and the spit bugs I can hear the grasshoppers telling stories.

'It's a DANCING lady, actually!' says Clementina who is making a lady from a yellow poppy.

'Yes, but why has she only got one leg?' says James.

'Because she's doing a pirouette,' says Clementina.

'No, cause she's a hoppy poppy!' says James and throws himself on the grass in giggles.

Kitty is sitting nearby with a cardboard box and Kes.

Kes sits on the middle of her finger in his dignity. Kitty is feeding him shining red raw slivers of meat. The meat has grey fluff on it. Kes takes the meat that is offered and tugs at it, and swallows, and blinks and opens his wide yellow eyes which have large pupils and his stare fixes itself on the next piece of meat.

I am leaning on my side watching him when we hear the watery sound of horses' hooves clopping in an uneven rhythm from the road that winds between the maple trees to Whitelaw. Kes hears the sound and his head bobs up and down. Three lurchers come bounding from behind the rhododendrons that edge the road and run towards us. Kes flutters his wings in alarm and gets caught up in the jessies Kitty has tied around his ankles. Kitty stands up.

'It must be them. I'll take him inside, I'd better, the dogs are frightening him.'

She walks up towards the house with Kes in the cardboard box and lifts it high above the noses of the interested dogs, and disappears inside the house, just as the clipping clopping hooves emerge from the trees and catch the sunlight.

There are three horses. A piebald, a scewbald and a shaggy grey. They are being ridden bareback by the beings who inhabit the Arabian Nights. We take the huge book from the high shelf in the schoolroom and turn the tracing paper that guards the carefully painted coloured pictures, that include gold. The colours are saffron and deep emerald, magenta, violet and turquoise, rich exotic colours that mingle with the ancient scent of the precious book.

Their hair is moving behind them in the wind, and tiny mirrors in their clothes glitter as they catch the light.

They trot near to where we are sitting and slow their horses to a walk. When they arrive they let go the reins.

Clementina stands up and says, 'Hello, Peter!' in her grown-up voice.

Peter has gold earrings and gold eyes, and when he opens his mouth to smile I see also he has a gold tooth. He is wearing a velvet purple waistcoat sewn with yellow thread and mirrors. He swings his leg across the front and slides off the horse frontways. He is barefoot. The lady has long yellow hair and a long sad face.

'Hello, Arianna,' says Clementina.

Arianna slides off the grey horse and her skirt rides up her long white legs. She smells of spices.

'Hello,' she says, and makes a musical jangling sound with her bracelets as she lands.

Her skirt is made of so many patches of so many colours, I am looking at it, and she says kindly, 'Do you like my skirt?' I nod, I like her skirt, and I like Peter's waistcoat and I look at him and his wide smile and his faraway eyes, and his beard and long brown hair, and think he must be Jesus. I am worried about his crucifixion but hope I can stand in the way of his smile so it shines on me.

James nudges me. 'Do you fancy him or what?'

I blush and glance at Peter, hoping he did not hear, and see him looking with long slow blinks into the air, and wonder if perhaps he is not all there either.

The other is a dark-haired man wearing jeans. He is still up on the piebald horse, and letting him eat the grass, with the reins loose. I like the way he sits up there and looks about. He is wearing three necklaces, Kitty walks towards us with the dogs bounding around her.

'Spring, come here!' says Peter.

Kitty is up close and when I see her as she looks at the dark-haired man, and I see her breathe, and I see her look at the ground then not know where to look and when I hear her voice crack and go funny when she says hello, and her legs shift uncomfortably from one to the other, by the forelegs of the black-and-white horse, I understand why it was that she risked so much in the kitchen gardens under the strawberry nets for a few squashed fruit.

'Let's go inside, you are expected!' says Clementina grandly. James and I cringe, but Peter and Arianna look happy and the dark-haired man slips down from his horse, smiles at Kitty, and Kitty falls into a dream.

We walk together towards the house. I turn back to look at their horses grazing on the front drive and wonder if at midnight they turn back to being rats. I take off my sandals and socks to be like Peter and feel the cold marble of the hall floor and then the soft stair carpet under my feet. I think his feet must be feeling the same as mine when we walk across the saloon and the shiny orange wood and hear the chandelier shiver at our step.

The drawing-room doors are open to allow the wind from the flowers to enter the house and fill the room with the warm breezes of the garden. The silk curtains billow a little, and the leaves of the lily are trembling. The sunlight makes squares of light on the aubusson rug, and lights up the little gold men, sailing boats across the Chinese cabinet.

Grown-ups are standing, and sitting in the large sofas and armchairs around the fireplace. There is the sound of ice clinking in tall jugs, filled with cherries and leaves of mint.

Uncle Finlay, collapsed in an armchair, pulls himself out with an effort, and stands up to introduce his friends.

He has a little chin on top of a big chin and a rosy smiling face. When he laughs his bottom chin quivers. He laughs a lot. But I carefully walk behind his chair in case he tickles me until it hurts.

I find myself next to Mama's armchair. She is shaking Peter's hand. I trace the yellow ribbon that ties a bunch of roses on the pattern of the curling arm.

'Darling, where are your shoes?'

I look at my feet and put my hand to my mouth, but before I can answer Peter says, 'Oh, I never like to wear them!' He smiles his glorious smile.

I notice Mama look down at his feet and nod politely. I

am holding my lips together to stop myself giggling when James motions to me from the open door. I slip behind the chair, behind the table, and through the double doors.

We race down both sides of the stone staircase, across the paving stones and out on to the grass. The sun is low but bright and the gentle wind is blowing the sweet scent of the yellow and orange azaleas across the lawn. The bees are still buzzing amongst them.

'Is he Jesus?' I ask James.

James looks from side to side, screws his mouth up, looks at me, raises one eyebrow, and nods.

'Will he get crucified?'

James looks at me, exasperated. 'Jesus doesn't get crucified every single time, you know!'

I am glad to hear it.

'Anyway, that's not what's important!'

'What's important then?'

'What's important is that the hippies are staying with Uncle Finlay at Whitelaw, and I heard Bob Cochrane say him and his brothers have built a huge tunnel in the barn.'

I stand and wait for the importance of this to touch me.

'Well, stupid, if we visit them, we can go in the TUNNEL!'

James climbs up on the balustrade and treading the frilly silver lichen, does an Indian War Dance, accompanied by an Indian War Cry.

*   *   *

I jump in and out of the squares of sunlight on the dining-room floor, Mrs McCready and Mrs McKay are clearing away the long and large lunch. The door into the garden is open, the roses and clematis wind around the staircase. I jump in and out of the doorway. There is a clutter of plates and cutlery and glasses empty and half full, cheese plates and pudding plates and plates piled with bones and half-eaten cabbage. I am amazed by the debris along the table that stretches from one end of the room to the other. Mrs McKay and Mrs McCready bustle along methodically clearing it, carrying trays through to the pantry. Trays of glasses, trays of small plates and then big plates. I skip along behind them and see it piled up on the pantry table ready to be washed, dried, then put away.

I climb up on to the table to see the great grey bell through the window that hangs above the kitchen. Mrs McCloud rings it every day at four o'clock. Once, she let me hang on the chain while she held me and rang it up and down. An immense sound rang through my body, I felt every particle of myself come apart, and be filled with the bell. She let me down and I went into a booming dream. I stood on the lino next to Doreen sounding a huge sound inside my body. I was still ringing when I got inside the lift to sit on the small fold-down seat in the corner and travel up to the nursery for my tea.

'Now come down, hen,' says Mrs McCready. 'Mrs

McKay widne like to find ye up there, get doon, there's a guid lass.'

When the great thick door of the pantry safe has been closed and all the silver returned to its cut-out shapes, cutlery shapes, square-dish shapes, round-dish shapes made of green felt, the dark glistening safe, with a door so thick that if you were shut inside you'd suffocate and no one would hear your cries, James says, when everything has been finished and cleared up and Doreen and Pauline have come for a 'wee bit of company', then they sigh and pull out chairs and sit down for their break.

Some pieces of the pudding have been left over, a dark-brown gateau with flakes of chocolate and plums inside, and Mrs McCready hands out the plates.

'Oh it's gorgeous!'

'Oh it's a grand flavour!'

The plums are preserved in brandy and I don't like the taste.

'Too strong for ye, hen?' says Mrs McCready kindly, pulling my plate towards her.

'Well, she can make a grand sweet, mind!' announces Mrs McKay.

'Well, ay, it'll be a' that mixin' and stirrin' she does,' says Doreen.

'How? Whit's she bin sayin' now?'

'Och no, it's nothin' at a'.'

'Now, Doreen, ah can tell that isne true.'

'Ah dinne think ah shid tell ye, like.'

'How?'

'Well, it's no ma business tae say.'

'Whit, say whit?'

'Well, whit she says aboot folk behind their back.'

'Oh ay, and whit's Lady Muck bein' sayin' now?'

Poor Mrs McCready sighs and looks out the window.

'Come on, hen. Oot wi'it.'

'It's maybe no' right te say.'

'Come on, if it's aboot me I need tae ken who ma friends are!'

'She said ye were hoity toity!'

Mrs McKay purses her lips together in a tight fury that makes lines around her mouth like a drawstring bag.

'If the wa'en wisne here ah'd ca' that woman by the name she deserves!'

'Well, we a' ken whit she's like!' says Doreen.

'Ah dinne even want ma sweet now,' says Mrs McKay pushing the plate away.

'Now, Morag, dinne take it tae heart, she's jist yin o' they folk who like makin' trouble, the best thing tae do is ignore it!' says Doreen.

'Ignore it! If anybody is hoity toity roond here it's Lady Muck o' the kitchen. That wumman is head cook and thinks she's the Lady hersel', och it makes me right sick, so it does!'

Suddenly they become quiet as we hear the chains of Mama's shoes clinking along the corridor. She comes into the pantry, and they all stand up, looking shy about their chocolate-covered plates.

'Oh please don't get up!' says Mama in her sweetest tone. 'Do sit down. I'm so glad you're having a nice break, you've done such a wonderful job. Thank you a thousand times.'

They nod and shuffle and only relax again when Mama has nodded sweetly and gratefully and closed the door again.

There are ten Cochrane children and they all live in one house. When we take them to church on Sunday, Mama calls after them in a high reedy voice as they scurry up the road, 'Thank you!' because they never say it, and, 'Honestly, those children have no manners!' as she winds up the window.

And my ambition is to have no manners like Hazel Cochrane, who turns a defiant face, and a cheeky mouth at anyone who tells her what to do.

And it is true that Bob Cochrane with his three brothers has built a terrifying tunnel in the hay bales. I can only see the dark entrance, but otherwise you'd never know.

We climb up the steps of straw and enter in. I shimmy along on my elbows.

The straw gets down my neck and into my clothes. I nose my way through in the darkness and the sweet smell, not knowing who I will meet. The tunnel goes around the whole barn. I am full of prickles and excitement.

'Hurry up!' says James from behind me. It's dark and warm and I just want to stay in there and breathe in the straw smell. Sounds are muffled. The tunnel winds and meanders.

We come out into the light. A long rope hangs from a beam. There is loose straw underneath, a long way down.

'Now jump!' says Bob.

James leaps out into the space at once and catches the rope and swings through the shafts of sunlight. I wait, terrified of having to go next.

'You next!' says Hazel and gives me a prod. 'Are you a scaredy?'

I nod.

'Ha! You're a scaredy! You're a scaredy!'

I breathe in a sigh, and wait for the rope to swing back. James has dropped into the loose straw below.

'You go next,' I say to Hazel.

'No, scaredies go first,' she says, 'go on!' and pushes me slightly. I wobble.

'Come on, Specky!' calls James from below. 'You can do it!'

'She's a scaredy-cat!' shouts Hazel. 'Your sister's a scaredy-cat and our Matthew can do it and he's only four!'

'She's not, actually!' says James. 'She's not, so there! Come on, Major, you've got wings!'

I realise James's honour is at stake.

'Yer a posh sissy!' says Hazel.

'She's braver than you!'

Oh no, now what? Hazel looks at me with disdain and without even looking leaps out into the void and catches the rope, I think quite by chance.

'Bet she can't do that!' Hazel taunts, her hair full of straw, with pink spit at the side of her mouth.

James scrambles up the vast distance of hay bales.

'Come on, Specks, show her! You've got to show her, or we're really stuck.'

It has become so tense I am frightened even to move. The space beneath sways back and forth. I am gripped.

'Scaredy! scaredy!' calls Hazel.

'Go! Go!' urges James.

'I can't,' I whimper.

But something happens. Suddenly some bright sunlight hits my face, and I feel my head filled with light. Something explodes inside me and I dive head first into the light-filled space, no rope and no idea of even landing, just nothing, just sunlight.

But I do land in the soft straw, and everyone is clapping, even Hazel. She crawls over to me in the straw and takes out her piece of chewing gum and offers it to me. I open my mouth and she puts it in, and then clambers up the hay bales to jump again.

Walking along the road back from Whitelaw, there is straw down my back that itches, and one lens lost down the hay bales from my glasses so I have to look through one eye, and we are in trouble because we have stayed out too long.

'We can tell her that Mr Cochrane had an accident and we had to wait for the ambulance.'

'But Mrs Cochrane is helping with the lunch tomorrow, then what if she sees Mrs Cochrane and she'd say it isn't true.'

'We could say that you really hurt your ankle, that it got twisted.'

'Sprained! We could say sprained.'

'Yes, OK, sprained.'

'And we had to go home really slowly,' James says as we jog along getting hotter and more itchy and I try to keep up.

'Oh never mind about it! Let's just be late! We're going to be late, that's all.'

I slow down to a walk, and pass my fingers through the crowds of campion growing pink from the fat green bulbs beneath the petals and white ragged robin, and purple vetch and long elegant shining buttercups.

The beech hedge becomes a fence and we can see down into the valley as the road winds along to the holly brae where tall trees rise up and the holly hangs down over the road.

James and I hold each other's hands and breathe quietly because this place is haunted with the ghosts of the wounded soldiers who carried the flag back from Flodden. And once, the uncles shot a bird here on a Sunday, and it screamed like a dying man.

The sun is low and the trees cast long shadows, streaks of lilac clouds are gathering on the horizon, their edges are yellow with light.

I feel something creep up my spine, and look at James in fright. He catches my fear and we both begin to run.

We run down the hill through the shadows and the strips of light, we run past the rows of dead weazels that hang on the fence, and past the thick fallen trunk that grows little orange mushrooms along its damp split. We run past the tall grey beeches and the rabbit holes, not stopping until we are round the corner and back in the sunlight.

'I felt one touch the back of my neck! I felt him creep his hand there.'

'I know, me too, I felt them all up and down my back.'

James makes a jerky movement in his spine.

We carry on through the pine trees and the scent of nettles, and along the road between the hills.

'Let's take a shortcut up the hill and across the ha-ha into the garden.'

We walk off the road across the tufty grass and the molehills. I can smell the freshly turned-over earth.

When we reach the brow of the hill we climb the grey stone ha-ha, and hoist ourselves up on to the grass. We watch the sun slip behind the dark hills. The lilac clouds have turned bright pink and crowd around the place the sun has left.

As the sky darkens something comes awake in the garden. A twilight wind blows from the trees. The birds begin to sing in a frenzy as we walk through the cherry orchard and when we reach the edge of the lawns the air is filled with their calls and chirrups. The fragrant air turns blue, and the flowers glow with the sunlight they've absorbed, setting free the colours in the cooling evening air.

The beings who sing in the green shadows of the day seem to be entering into the wide-open spaces as the night begins to fall. Their secret joy and their mystery is infectious to us and we fall into the quietness of that other world, as we are filled by their presence, for they too are longing for us to join them.

We crawl down amongst the fallen twigs and the periwinkles and watch each other's pale faces grow obscure in the dimming light.

'We've got to go! We've got to go!' says James suddenly, waking us from our dream. 'We're really late, we're in hot water!'

We run across the lawn and past the silent fountain, along the balustrade and up the stone steps into the music-room passage.

'I think it's cold water,' I say, as we run through the curtain past the sitting room and climb the wide front stairs. 'It seems like it's cold water to me,' as the feeling of dread and Doreen's fierce eye comes into my mind.

We get to the top of the stairs and hold hands through the dark corridor.

'Well, people say hot. Trouble is hot, that's why, they don't say we'll be in cold water, do they?'

'They could, though, they might.' We walk around the Egg and the nursery is in listening distance. It is well past our bed-time.

We walk along the Nursery Corridor through the door and around the screen covered in pictures that Grandmama made.

We stand still and look up at Doreen. Her hands are on her hips, her eyes are hard, and her mouth is a thin line.

'What time do you call this!' she shouts.

The air cracks and turns cold.

It is nearly lunch-time. I sit on the nursery sofa, with my knitting needles and green wool. Mrs McCready has been teaching me plain and pearl. I wind the wool around the needles and try to pull it through to make a stitch, but the loop gets lost somewhere, and I try to find it among all the other loops.

Hugh toddles around the edge of the sofa and rests his chin on the cushion. Sometimes when he looks at me, it is as though he has awoken from a beautiful dream, and does not know where he is. And in his eyes that look into mine is a question. 'What are we doing here?' they say. 'What *are* we doing here?' I can only hoist him up on to the sofa and point to the teddy bears on my knitting pattern.

The radio is playing and Don McLean sings goodbye to his American Pie. I know about Americans. They come and stay in a crowd during the shooting season. Then Mr Knap arrives and the dark-red livery with gold buttons is unwrapped from tissue paper for the footmen, and the heating is switched on. Davie Stirling, the road sweeper from Whitelaw, puts on his kilt and his sporran and walks

round the dining-room table after dinner playing the
bagpipes. We listen over the Egg.

Doreen comes in with the tray that has been sent up in
the lift from the kitchen. James is dancing about behind
her.

'We're having shepherd's pie!' sings James, to rhyme
with the American pie on the radio. 'And, guess what?'

'What?'

'Rhubaaarb!'

We sit around the table. Kitty is eating more often in
the dining room and today is the big lunch downstairs.

James shifts round on his seat and sings to the music.
Doreen switches off the radio.

'Will you sit still!'

James still bounces about.

'What's wrong with you?'

'I can't help it, it's in my head!'

'Don't answer me back!'

James tries to sit still but his legs still jig about.

'I'd like to get a strait-jacket for you!'

James makes a disgusted face.

'All the hippy gippies are coming today,' he says with
his mouth full.

'Don't speak with your mouth full!'

James looks at me and raises his eyes to the ceiling.

Doreen sees, and leans over and smacks him.

'And don't be insolent!'

'Can't do anything round here,' says James quietly, looking at his plate. Doreen ignores him.

When we have finished we say, 'Please may I get down?' and Doreen says, 'Mind you behave. Pauline and I are helping in the pantry so don't get in anyone's way. You can go downstairs and say hello to the guests, but don't make a nuisance of yourselves, do you hear?'

We nod, and race out of the nursery.

I am crouched in the sweetie cupboard. A crack in the door lights up the cardboard boxes on the floor, and baskets of string and Mama's secateurs, and the two tall jars of Hawick balls and Berwick cockles on the top shelf. I didn't mean to be in here when they came in, but James said, 'Go and hide and I'll find you', so I went and hid, but sometimes I hide and wait and wait and when I finally get tired of waiting, I go and find him and he says, 'Hello, Specky, what you doing?' and laughs a laugh with mischief in it and I know that he never was intending to come and find me. Maybe now is one of those times, but I didn't mean to be here when they came in and started saying private things to each other, but they came in so fast, I got trapped. I can smell the cardboard boxes and brown paper. I am frightened of the cold in Mama's voice.

'I'll not have you drunk at this lunch, John!'

'Just let me be,' Papa says in a tired voice.

'I don't want you collapsing on the table at the end of the meal for everyone to see!'

'Oh, leave me alone,' Papa growls.

'I try to keep things going, I try, I try,' says Mama in a voice that is sad.

'As long as it all *looks* all right, everything's fine,' Papa growls again.

'I'm doing my best!' she says in a helpless tone. 'I can't do any more than that.'

'Oh yes, we all know that you do your best, we all know that!'

Mama is angry. 'And what do you do? What do you do? Drunk and hopeless, falling about all over the place for all the servants to see, what help are you? And I don't know how we'll get the Americans to come this year after last year's performance.'

A jar of Copydex behind my head suddenly falls off the shelf and bangs against the door. I hold my breath, horrified by the thought of being found in here listening.

'Oh say it, why don't you say it, what a hopeless pathetic man you married . . .' he shouts.

'Be quiet!'

'I don't care,' murmurs Papa.

'I know you don't.'

'I don't care about you, I don't care about any of it!'

I hear him collapsing into a chair. The springs creak.

'I don't want you at this lunch, do you hear? I'm not having the whole county seeing you like this! Stay in here, do you hear? I'll say you're ill or something.'

'Yes, yes, yes, say what you want, as long as it all looks OK, that's all right with you, never mind that the whole place is falling apart, never mind the death duties and debts. Never mind that as long as it looks . . .' His voice trails off.

Mama says in a slow, cold voice, 'I do my best, I can do no better, and I would appreciate some help from you.'

I hear her shoes clinking towards the door, she opens it, turns to him and says, 'Stay in here!' and closes the door. I hear Papa give a shivering sigh.

When I hear Papa snoring I gently open the door of the sweetie cupboard and slip out. I close the sitting-room door quietly and walk past the striped sofa.

I can hear a gathering of people in the drawing room, noises of laughing, joking and clinking. I walk through the saloon. The drawing-room door is open.

I walk into the room and stand behind an armchair to look around for James.

A tall man in a tweed jacket smoking a pipe through his moustache talks to a lady in a geranium-pink cardigan and pearls. He slides his eyes sideways sometimes to see the man in shining purple trousers strumming a pretend guitar by the window.

The hippies have multiplied. Their clothes are colourful. A small group stand by him, sipping drinks.

The man in a red bandana wears sunglasses. A lady in a blue suit smiles politely at him, but when she looks away her eyes are scared. She turns to a man in a brown tie who begins to tell her a story and she puts an interested expression on her face with her eyebrows raised. By the centre table Mama is standing, laughing and talking among three ladies who all have hairstyles. When they move the hair stays in place.

Others are spilling into the pink landscape of the morning room where mandarin ducks swim among the reeds.

Clementina is busy fetching drinks from the drinks cupboard behind a tall lily.

The dark-haired man sits cross-legged on the square sofa opposite the fireplace. Beside him is a gentle-looking woman with long curly hair and silver hoops in her ears. A lilac scarf is tied around her head like a pirate and her dress has pink and violet flowers on it. It is thin material and beneath I can see her bare arms, and the shape of her bosoms. The dark-haired man gazes at her and they laugh and talk. She has lips the same colour as her face. She is stroking his forearm.

I look around for Kitty and see her at the fireplace with her back to them. She is busily tracing the curves and spirals carved into the grey marble. She is concentrating so hard that she doesn't notice as I come and stand beside her. There is a determined look on her face and her lips are pressed together as she follows each curve with her forefinger. I join in and her finger meets mine along a curve. She looks down at me then. The light in her eyes has changed colour from yellow light to a pale-blue mist on a hill. She turns away, she does not want me to see the pale-blue mist.

James comes and pokes me in the back.

'Hello, Specky, I've been looking for you high and low!'

'Liar!'

'No, honest,' he says. 'Come on, let's go!'

He takes my hand and pulls me through the talking people. I look back at Kitty. She has sat down on the hearth and watches the garden out the window.

We walk into the saloon hand in hand. Clementina is explaining to Pete, 'You must never sit down on these chairs, they are very delicate and very precious!' He is nodding.

We run through to the dining-room where Mrs McKay and Mrs McCready are arranging silver dishes on the hotplate.

'Come on,' says James.

'Where to?'

'I've got a plan.'

'What?'

'Quick!'

'Where do you want to go, though?'

He is pulling me by the arm.

'To the kitchen!'

'Why?'

'Because!'

'Yes, but what for?'

'OK, I'll give you one clue, the pulley lift!'

The pulley lift is the place Mrs Fergus puts the steaming dishes, and pulls on the rope, so Mrs McKay can take them out in the pantry, to serve them in the dining-room.

He is dragging me by the sleeve down the back stairs, round the grille of the big iron lift, that takes people all the way up to the attics.

'What about the pulley lift?'

'I'm going to get in it!'

Light streams into the kitchen through the tall windows next to the ceiling. The copper pans and jelly moulds that hang along the wall from the pulley lift to the far end light up in the sunlight. They are never used. Inside they have turned pale green in the cracks. It's arsenic, James says, and if you even lick it, your tongue goes black, your skin goes yellow and your eyes pop out of your head. Then you die and nothing can save you.

The cooks are bustling about beside the steaming pans, and Mrs McCloud is wiping down the centre table with long slow wipes.

'Och, Mary, dinne ferget the vegetable dish.'

'No eatin' meat!' exclaims Mrs Cowe lifting steamed plums from the pan, and shaking her head.

'No eatin' meat, no cuttin' their hair . . .'

'No gettin' wed, frae what ah've heard!'

Mrs McCloud picks up the dish with leeks in cheese and mushroom sauce for the ones 'who dinne eat meat' and walks along towards the pulley lift.

'Well, gid afternin!' she says to us. 'Now dinne get in the road today.' She looks across at Mrs Fergus. 'Be sure and dinne get on the wrong side o' things today.' She gives us a knowing look.

'Specky can pull the lift up!' says James.

'Ay, OK then, hen!' She places the leeks on the shelf.

When she turns round, James checks the other two absorbed in their tasks and quickly lifts himself up and clambers into the shelf below.

'Quick! Pull!' he whispers from inside the lift. He is hunched over tight like a ball.

'Quick, before they see!'

I begin to pull desperately and see him pass my eyes and the lift travel upwards. I hear the lift hatch being opened on the floor above. A voice shouts down. I stop pulling.

It is Mrs McKay.

'I'd like tae remind ye that the Lady ordered a vegetarian dish fer they that dinne eat meat!'

Mrs Fergus slams down the pan and marches towards the pulley lift.

'And ah'll have ye know that I dinne need to be telt ma job!' she shouts up the lift shaft.

'Well, if ye dinne need tae be telt yer job, I suggest ye dae it!'

'Ah dinne ken whae ye think yer speakin' tae!'

I am standing by the rope not able to pull it but knowing that James is stuck between the floors.

'Oh ah ken fine whae ah'm speakin' tae.'

'Do you now, and is it you who's runnin' this hoose, like?' Mrs Fergus has gone white with anger. 'Tellin' folk that know whit they're aboot, their ain business! Ye' like tae think yer somebody, that's yer trouble!'

'Ah ken fine whae ah am, and whit ma job is!'

'Then why don't ye do it, and pu' this lift up, and see whit's in it, ye stupid besom!' shouts Mrs Fergus.

'I BEG your pardon!'

'You heard!'

'Well, I've never been so insulted!'

'Ay, well, enjoy it!'

'Ah'm no' pulling this lift anywhere, till ah get an apology.'

'The dish is in the lift, it's you who shid apologise!'

'I widne apologise tae you!'

But the rope begins to travel upwards as she pulls it from above.

Mrs Fergus walks back to the stoves in disgust, clattering the pans and muttering to Mrs Cowe. Mrs McCloud continues slowly to wipe the long table, shaking her head to herself.

As the lift reaches the pantry floor, there is a clunk, then a loud scream, and the sound of crockery smashing to pieces. The cooks turn round together and look at the pulley lift, then at each other. I run out of the kitchen, along the passage, up the stairs and into the pantry.

Mrs McCready is kneeling on the floor, picking up the broken pieces of leeks in cheese and mushroom sauce. Mrs McKay is leaning on the table with her hand on her heart, saying, 'Oh whit a fright, ah'll never get o'er it!'

And Doreen has James by the shoulders and is shaking him so violently I think his head will fall off.

'Whit are ye aboot? Whit were ye thinkin' of? Ah'm takin' you upstairs, ma lad, and whit a hidin' ah'm goin' tae give you!'

She pulls him by the hand and out the door. He looks at the floor all the while.

The pantry falls silent.

'Well, Morag,' says Mrs McCready, leaning back on her heels, 'somebody'll hae tae go doonstairs and ask them fer another dish!'

Mrs McKay suddenly draws herself up. 'Well, ah can tell you this! It'll no' be me, fer as long as ah live ah'm no' speakin' to that wumman until ah get an apology!'

James is sent to bed and I spend the rest of the lunch in the pantry, and help with the washing up and putting away. At last the dining room is empty and I ask Mrs McCready if she will unlock the door so I can go into the garden.

'Are ye sure yer allowed, hen?'

I nod, and she opens it.

I walk down the stone steps on to the lawn. There are chirrups and long trills calling from the trees. Underneath these sounds I hear a cuckoo. I walk round the box hedge. The sky is overcast.

At the bottom of the drawing-room steps, on the low flat ledge of the sun-dial, I see Kitty sitting alone.

The stone step is covered in dry yellow moss and lichen, silver blue. She crouches over with her head bent down and her arms wrapped around her knees.

I sit on the low flat step beside her, and feel huge sad

feelings floating round her and through the air, they start to fill me up and I see a dark lake deep in the ground.

Kitty turns her head without unclasping her knees. She looks at me sideways and her eyes are red.

'Are you crying?' I whisper very close so as not to disturb her. She shakes her head.

I know that this is not a falling-down hurting-yourself pain. This is a wide-open longing pain that stretches off as far as the blue hills and seems never to end. It is the streak of blue left over in the summer sky when the sun has gone, plaintive like the peewits crying over the moor. It is an empty space inside Kitty.

I put my arm on her shoulder and rest my chin there. She sniffs and sighs. We sit together in silence for some time. The breeze is blowing the wisps of hair around her forehead.

Two blackbirds start a quarrel in the hedge. The commotion dies down, and Kitty is quietly crying. I sit close beside her and feel her tears come in little throbs.

I put my arm around her shoulder and she leans her head on my neck. I feel her tears drip inside my collar.

'What shall I do?' she whispers through them.

I don't really know. 'Maybe just wait till it gets better.'

'It won't get better,' she says.

'Why not?'

She doesn't answer.

*   *   *

After a while a cold breeze begins to blow and we get up
from the step and walk slowly up the stairs holding hands
and through the drawing-room door. The room is quiet,
everything back in its place. Kitty lets go my hand and
glances over to the sofa where she sat, the woman with
skin-coloured lips, and looks quickly at the floor. There is
not even a dimple in the cushion. She opens the tall door
into the saloon. There is a chill in the air. As we walk
through the double doors on to the landing I feel a great
monster inhabits the space between the staircase. There
are dark shadows in the corners of the windows and no
sound is coming out of the sitting-room. It is silent like a
cavern. We approach it and listen, the silence is fierce.

'Well, drinking won't solve anything,' says Mama's
voice at last.

There is the silence again. Papa has been swallowed
by the monster that lives in the great gaping space
down the middle of the staircase and that is why he
can't talk.

Then I hear his little whisper.

'There's no money, there's only debts and death duties,
its hopeless!'

There is a cry in his voice and it sounds like china
breaking on a stone floor, it has cracked open.

'Nothing is hopeless, pull yourself together!'

Mama's voice has a raw red streak in it, but the monster

does not swallow her too. And I see that she is trying to pull Papa out of the monster's mouth. I turn to Kitty and she tugs me by the hand. We run back up the stairs and into the room that will be mine when she has gone to boarding school.

'It's all right, Specky. Don't worry.'

I can feel that my eyes are wide open and looking for her. We sit on the window seat and look out the window.

'Are we going to leave here?'

'I don't know. Maybe, but don't you worry about it, these are grown-up worries, you are too little.'

'Why has Papa been swallowed by that monster?'

'There isn't a monster, it's all right.'

'And she's been carryin' on a' that time, and she's never breathed a word o' it tae me.'

'And how did ye first ken, like?'

'Oor Maurcen saw them in Alnwick.'

They shake their heads.

'Ye could say as she did it a' behind yer back.'

Doreen nods. 'Not one word.'

'And is it . . .' Mrs Fergus mouths a word then nods and lifts her eyebrows.

Doreen nods. They all shake their heads. Mrs Cowe deliberately stubs out her cigarette. There is a silence.

They lean towards each other around the small red

table at the end of the kitchen. Light streams in through the tall window that looks out into the yard.

The space between them is tight with disapproval, but two figures slip out from inside it and dance freely around the ceiling. I think one of them is Pauline.

'And whit dis yer mither say, like?'

'Ah'd like tae ken mair whit *her* mither has tae say!' states Mrs Fergus.

They look at Doreen. 'Och, ay well, she's beside hersel', he's right keen on the lassie, ye ken. There's nought tae do aboot it! Whit's done is done!'

'Whit a lassie, ay?'

'She seems right quiet an a'.'

'Ye widne think . . .'

'And where . . . ye ken . . .' There are a few mouthed words, and the conversation continues with the exchange of scandalised expressions.

'Ay well, these quiet ones . . .' Mrs Cowe nods her head towards me. I am startled by being made suddenly visible. I have been playing by the legs of the long table with an orange Dinkie car.

'Off you go and tell Mrs McCloud her tea's getting cold,' says Doreen.

I leave my car by the leg of the table that stretches down the centre of the kitchen and go through into the long black passage that Mrs McCloud mops from the chapel to the scullery every single day. I run to find her in the gloom.

She has reached the servants' hall and sways gently back and forth with her mop.

'Your tea's getting cold, Doreen says.'

'By, it's close today!' she says, pushing back a stray white hair and looking down at me. They say that Mrs McCloud has gypsy blood, I take this to mean the donkey Gypsy. I think it may be her dark-brown eyes.

James runs out of the gloom with his arms outstretched, humming like an aeroplane. He makes wet footprints down the passage.

'See that brother of yours?' she says smiling. 'He's going to get a skelping!'

She picks up the mop bucket and mop, and slowly sways towards the kitchen. James runs up and down around us.

'And I suppose you'll be wanting Coca-cola?'

'Yes,' we say together.

She stops at the store cupboard.

'Och, ah canny stand this heat!' she says unlocking the door and bending down under the shelf to fetch the bottles. She opens them and hands them to us.

The window into the moat is open and lets in a little breeze as we pass by. Mrs McCloud stops to stand by it.

'Och, whit's a body to do in this heat!'

'They can go out!' shouts Doreen from the end of the kitchen. 'Tell them they can go out!'

But we don't need a telling, and climb out the window into the moat, clutching our bottles of Coke.

We climb up between the hedge and the balustrade and into the flower-bed, full of silver leaves and lady's mantle. We take off our sandshoes and run across the soft grass. The air is hot.

We sit on the mossy edge of the fountain with our feet in the cool water and listen to the sound of the spray, sipping the warm Coke from the green glass bottles. But the Coke is sticky on the sides of our mouths and attracts the wasps. One comes to lick the sweetness from the edge of James's lips. He waits, very still, trying to watch it down the edge of his nose.

We leave the bottles by the fountain and run to the trees. Under the copper beech the light turns pale pink through the purple leaves. The long grass tickles our feet. We sit breathing under the trees and now and again the shadows and dots of light gently tremble. We don't talk today. We have been drawn into a silent deep place. The close air dazes our minds, and the sweet-smelling shadows soothe our bodies.

'Let's go to the tree house!' James whispers.

We set off through the cherry orchard, careful of our

bare feet among the broken twigs. The tiny fruit are beginning to redden. We reach the ha-ha. I muster the courage to jump down, on to the grass.

The sun has dried it to straw. The sheep shit is baking, James takes a stick to open the black crust and see the green grass inside. The sheep are grazing slowly on the hills, looking naked with big heads. The burn winds along at the bottom of the valley.

We run down the hill and across the road and down to the burn over the straw grass. We fall over the ridge, and roll down across the bumps and the sheep shit. I lie in the warm grass at the bottom, hearing the gentle tinkle of the water and watching the hot blue sky.

James comes with his hands cupped and releases the cold water on to my face, I scream and gasp and jump up. He laughs.

The water is cool, and it runs red because of the earth. We splash in it and build bridges with the stones. We follow the burn along, being careful of our feet on the slippy smooth stones and jaggy rocks. Skylarks dip up and down, and pigeons call from the woods. There are nooks and crannies for the trout to hide under. Sunlit water shadows ripple the overhanging leaves.

We stand still and respectfully when we see the dipper. He flies on to a moss-covered stone in the middle of the running water. He looks at us with his beady eye, and flies away. He lives under the bridge. This is his stretch of water.

The bank inclines steeply upwards and over us towers the great tree that stretches up to the sky. Its immense tangled roots are exposed. This is the tree house. This is not an everyday place.

James and I look at each other. We must climb up the bank. It is almost a mud slide. James climbs up first and lies on the ground holding on to the root so I can catch his foot and climb up his body. We reach the entrance of the roots. We wait, and then we enter.

Inside the tree house is red. The roots are red, the floor is red. Rabbits live here and leave their droppings. The tree stretches up above our heads and we are held in the depths of its great presence. It fills us with awe and quietness. We climb into its deepest places, deep in the heart of the tree, and the magic is so strong we can do nothing but sit listening. For a long time we sit in the strange silence that absorbs all sound.

Slowly we become aware that it is time to leave, and get up together. We emerge from the red shadows into the green light, both of us covered in earth. In the distance we hear the four o'clock bell.

As we cross the lawn, a cloud brings a sudden shower, which darkens the garden. We run to collect our soggy sandshoes and the rain makes streaks down our skin, stained with the earth. As we walk up the back stairs I watch James' stripy legs take two steps at a time.

When we reach the nursery the sky outside has turned a strange greenish yellow.

Doreen is sewing name tags on to socks. We climb up on to the toy box to look at the clouds coming swiftly now, in banks of grey and glowering with an eerie light. Sheets of rain hit the window and we gasp.

'We could've been caught in that!'

We beg Doreen to open the window. The rain subsides a little, and the greenish light returns. Then suddenly a violet light cracks out of the sky and enters the ground. A great sound rumbles from under the earth and we stand leaning on the windowsill watching the display, as the lightning flashes and the thunder rolls, and the fields of grass are flooded, and the raindrops hit the windowsill and splash up on our faces until the mud is all washed away.

The sounds fade, and the sky closes. Doreen sighs and stretches.

'Now, you two, bath-time. Heavens above, look at the state of you!'

The fire in the hearth is glowing. Mama is writing letters at her desk. A piece of wood falls into the centre and a flame leaps up the chimney.

'What does that spell?'

I am lying on the sheepskin rug, making words with the red-and-white ivory letters.

'It doesn't spell anything.'

'But will you read it?'

Kitty sighs.

'It just says GWIKNG.'

I am thrilled that my letters make this sound. I lay down another series that stretches across the hearth, and into the white rug.

'What does *this* spell?'

'It doesn't spell anything. It's nonsense.'

'But what does it sound like?'

'I can't read it, it's too long.'

'This bit then, just read what this bit is.'

'GMBOLTHLNX.'

'Does it say that?'

'Yes, but it isn't a word.'

'Will you make me a word?'

There is a knock at the door. Mama looks up from behind her desk.

'Come in.'

Pauline pokes her head tentatively round the door.

'Excuse me, Lady Mary?'

'Yes, Pauline, do come in.'

Mama gives us a look that says would you leave us, please.

'Why are we going out?' I ask outside the door.

'Because they would like a private word.'

'What is a private word?'

'It's a secret conversation.'

We wander down the music-room passage.

I feel sure I would like a private word myself.

Mama is still at her desk when we return to the warmth. She looks up at Kitty.

'Well,' she sighs, and looks back to her papers. 'We're losing Pauline.'

I see Pauline slip through a gap in the floor, and reach for Kitty's hand.

Kitty whispers, 'It's OK, she's getting married. I know because she told me.'

We sit down again by the flames. The angel swings back and forth under the clock. Mama continues to write. Kitty has fallen into a silence. I look at her and she smiles. But in her green eyes I see a black-and-white horse pulling a caravan over a brow, and in the space it leaves an aching flute sound.

I reach up to her ponytail and stroke it down her back.

'Would you like a hairbrush?'

She shakes her head.

'Shall I tell you a secret, can you keep it?'

I nod my head vigorously. 'Is it a private word?'

'Yes,' she says.

She motions me to come close and I kneel down on the rug with my ear close to her mouth. She whispers something but her breath tickles my ear.

'I can't hear, say it again!'

'She's going to have a baby!'

'Like baby Jesus?' I blurt out loud and clap my hands over my mouth. She looks at me, exasperated, and looks quickly at Mama, who is absorbed in her writing.

'Yes, like baby Jesus.'

The rain is beating hard against the window in the nursery and the wind rattles the panes, the house is being buffeted by the gust. The sky is slate grey. Doreen is still sorting, folding, and sewing. She looks tired.

James is moving the folded jerseys into roads and streets to drive his Dinkie cars along. Doreen stands up suddenly and lifts him on to his feet by the wrist, and smacks his hand.

'I've just sorted those!'

James looks surprised.

'Out you go, you too, madam.' She lifts me on to my feet by the wrist. 'I've had enough of you under my feet. Go and play along the corridor!'

As we walk along by the Egg she shouts after us, 'And *don't* go up to the attics.'

'She's *unfair!*' says James, and kicks the wainscot, then walks nonchalantly straight to the bottom of the attic stairs.

We stand in the dark recess at the mouth of the black stairs that climb to an even greater depth.

It smells musty, I feel clogged up with the dark.

'She said not to, though,' I whisper, scared to speak aloud in the gloom.

'How will she know? We can just sneak up and go exploring and then come down.'

'Well, but I don't like going up there anyway, I don't like it up there, James, let's not go.'

'Yes, come on, Specks, come on, come on, come on.'

I don't want to be left down here alone and I can't go back to the nursery without James, and I can't persuade him not to go, so I follow him up, step by step, into the terrifying presence of the attic.

We reach the top stair and the hair on the back of my neck is prickling.

'Come on,' says James, excited, 'let's go down this corridor.'

I walk gingerly behind him, feeling the bristling of inhuman presences crowding around us. Strange eerie feelings and unfelt longings, cold rages, and forgotten loves that seem to throng the abandoned rooms. Hungry ghosts cram the air and attempt to suck our life, our child light from around our bodies. I feel stifled and breathless.

'I can't stand it!' I whisper, 'I can't stand it, I have to go!' I say, almost in a sob.

'No, no, Specky. Look! It's OK, don't panic, look!' He opens the door into a room and we see the raindrops glistening in a stray beam of light. I run over to the window to see the garden from so high above. The fountain is being filled by the rain. I think of the great big toad who lives in the drain, sitting there in his ponderous silence and blinking and swallowing as the water flows around him. The sunlight disappears.

'Look,' says James from behind me. He has opened a trunk and is fanning out a feather fan. It has long black feathers which glisten with a green metallic sheen. He has unwrapped it from tissue paper. I take it from him reverently and stroke the long feathers and the tortoise-shell handle.

'Look, there are more.'

And there are. A box full of carefully wrapped fans, one yellow ivory with carved processions of tiny elephants and trees, another gaudy black and red that opens out to reveal an enormous crimson rose and black tassels, a fan of blue feathers and a carefully painted Chinese fan with a scene of a man and his wife going home along a road. I am mesmerised and absorbed.

When I look round, James is gone. He is hiding. Maybe he is hiding. Don't panic. He is just pretending.

I walk to the door, I daren't let myself know I am alone. But when I see the black corridor and feel the sucking, whistling presence of the attic bristling round my skin I cannot contain my terror and scream, 'JAMES!'

He pops his head out from a room further down the corridor.

'Don't get your knickers in a twist, Specks, I'm only here, and just look what I've found!'

He steps out from behind the door to reveal himself wearing a heavy army greatcoat. His head looks little between the wide shoulders and the skirt of the coat spreads around him on the floor.

'Good, aye?' he says, showing me a side view as though it is a perfect fit. 'And guess what? It's his!'

He steps back through the door. I hear his voice.

'Look, there's his hat here.'

He comes around the door again, wearing the peaked cap down over his eyes.

'It's what?'

'It's Great Uncle Jim's, it says on the trunk.'

Great Uncle Jim was Grandpapa's brother, he went to the First World War and never came home. There are brown photographs of his long sad face in the library, standing in his plus fours wth a gun, and Grandpapa when he was young too.

'I know what!' James says with sudden glee. 'Let's play soldiers!'

'NO! I don't want to be here, and I don't want to play soldiers and I HATE you!'

I am slightly surprised by the outburst and stand still in the clarity of my own shock.

'All right then,' says James, and goes back inside the room not the slightest bit perturbed.

'Oh Specky, look!' he says from inside again. 'Come here. Come here. Look!'

He is so excited that I run into the room. The walls are covered in faded rosebuds and the ceiling slants towards the window. James is pointing outside. The trees are lit up golden yellow by the sun and stand out from the slate-grey sky still full of rain.

'Can you see it?' says James, squealing in delight. 'Look, can you see?'

With my face up against the window, I can see it behind the trees, a clear strong double rainbow.

'Oh, I've got to see it, I've got to see it,' says James, rushing from the room.

I follow helplessly. 'Where are you going? Where are you going now?'

He runs down another corridor and turns a corner.

When I catch him up he is standing at the foot of the stepladder.

'I know where the key is!' he says, jumping up and down, 'I know where it is, I saw Papa.'

He climbs up the ladder and retrieves the key from the door lintel and holds it out for me to see.

I know I cannot protest, that nothing will stop him, but I also know that going up on to the roof is a grave and terrible crime, strictly forbidden even by Papa.

James has the key in the lock of the pyramid-shaped skylight. The rain makes a tapping sound on the glass, and the drops drip down in shadows on the pale-green steps.

He pulls back the skylight on its runners, and the drops hit his face. He holds his head back smiling a wide smile, and lets out a scream of joy, then runs up the steps in a hurry and out on to the wide flat roof. I step out more carefully. The roof is slippery and shining wet, reflecting the sky, and from behind the dovecot at the end of the avenue to the blue hills in the distance stretches the magnificent triumph of the rainbow.

We scream at it together, scream and scream, and do wild dances in the puddles and around the tall chimneys that make the roof a village of streets and alleys. We dance around the tower of the tall gold weathercock, and shout wordless triumph across the tops of the trees and the fields and the endless distance.

Only when the sun returns behind the clouds and the sky glowers greenish grey do we suddenly become cold in the wind and rain, and notice we are soaked. And only when we have returned through the skylight and stand at the foot of the stairs again, do we realise that people playing in the top corridor don't end up with clothes that stick to their skin and make them shiver.

'I know what.'

'What?' I say, my teeth chattering.

'We can go into the wash room and put them through the mangle.'

So we drip along the corridor leaving footsteps on the dusty linoleum and go through the white door with wiggly glass windows into the wash room. It has two skylights and the rain patters on the glass.

We peel off our clothes and stand hopping from one foot to the other on the wooden slats in front of the two low enamel sinks and carefully wind each item through the mangle that is fixed between them. James helps them through and I wind, and the water is squeezed out. Then we wind them around the hot pipes and they begin to steam. We hop around naked trying to keep warm.

The door is open and I feel a sinking feeling when I hear the crank and hum of the lift getting ready to make its journey from the kitchen to the nursery floor.

'It's the lunch, James!'

James screws his lips up to the side.

'Yes. Hmmm, it is, isn't it.'

'Doreen will be out looking for us.'

We hear the lift land and the gates go back.

'Better be quick!' says James, unwinding the clothes and putting them on anyway.

Trying to get in between the legs of the wet trousers is an uncomfortable task, especially when my heart is beating and my fingers are trembling.

I buckle up my sandals and feel horribly damp.

'She might not notice,' says James.

We run around the corridors away from the back stairs and the lift, and race down the little stairs that lead into the dark alcove. Doreen is coming along the corridor.

'Didn't you hear me?' she says, catching sight of us in the gloom.

'No,' we say from the darkness. 'We were playing in the cushions.'

As I follow her along the corridor, I feel as if my body doesn't fit together. It is wobbly. I wobble along behind her into the round sky light of the Egg, and into the brightly lit nursery.

It has stopped raining.

Doreen turns round to us. Her mouth opens and she starts breathing long breaths. I look down at the still wet and wrinkled shirt, the trousers dark with damp.

'*What* is this? *What* is this?' she says, her eyes widening, fingering James's damp cuff and my wet shirt.

'You're soaked through!'

'The window was open,' says James hopefully.

'WINDOW! WINDOW! I know what you've done!' she says with a rasping voice, catching us both by the wrists in one hand and lifting us on to our tip-toes.

'I know where you've been!' and whack! her hand comes down hard on our suspended bodies. Whack! whack! the blows getting harder, stinging through the wet clothes. Whack! whack! She hits us all over our legs, our arms, our backs, our fronts. We shout and yell out, calling her to stop, that we're sorry, and even James is crying and sobbing with the pain and the terror of her uncontrolled fury.

'You're not to do that again! Not to! Not to!' She is almost sobbing herself, and as she lets us go I see a terror fall out of her eye and in the same moment I see an image in my mind's eye of James and me lying crushed and broken on the gravel outside the porch.

I feel a change. It turns cold. The wood pigeons roo coo in the damp air. The leaves turn dark green and the grass stops growing. Something has fallen away from underneath.

Inside the rooms darken, and the presences chased into

the black shadows by the summer sunlight begin to roam the corridors once more.

In the nursery Doreen still sews. The sofa is piled with grey socks and vests and pants and shirts, those done, those still to do. There is a blazer with a blue crest and a cap and a striped blue-and-indigo tie that Doreen has taught James how to tie. He stands in front of the long nursery mirror with his new cricket bat doing pretend shots, shouting, 'That's an over! That's a duck!' and standing up and saying, 'Well done, sir,' to his own reflection. He is excited and I am excited too because he is.

The big trunk is open on the linoleum floor, it has wooden ridges. Everything is being neatly fitted into it.

He turns to me. 'Bowler, bowl!'

I pretend to bowl him a ball, he hits it and it crashes through the window pane. He makes the sound of the crash. Doreen looks tired. She gets up, takes the bat from James, who lets it go with his eyebrows raised, and puts it in the trunk.

'Off you go now, and play.' She motions to the nursery door.

Hugh is busy slowly examining a hair in the black sheepskin rug. James and I run from the room, happy to play 'He' round the Egg.

*   *   *

When the trunk is ready, it is carried along the corridor by Stuart and Mr Chisolm. They take it down in the lift and put it on the square trailer Mr Chisolm puts the logs in when he fills the log baskets. They wheel it out the side door and put it in the back of the Zephyr, long before it is time for James to go. It sits in the car outside the front porch all morning, and when we come out the front door later on it is waiting for him in the car.

Papa is driving him to the station, and Clementina and Kitty and Mama are here to say goodbye.

James is jumping about with excitement and I jump up and down with him.

'Darlings, do calm down, please. It's not very nice hearing all that screaming.'

James's eyes are glistening and bright. There is a mist on the avenue in the far distance and we can't see to the dovecot. The house seems still.

'Say goodbye now.'

James refuses to kiss anyone and jumps in beside Papa and blows kisses instead.

'Bye, you rotten apple,' he says to Clementina.

'Bye, cat gut,' she says.

'Bye, baboon bum,' he says.

'Please, darlings!' says Mama, pursing her lips. James laughs ecstatically because Clementina can't get the last word.

'Bye.'

'Bye.'

Everyone waves and shouts 'Bye'.

It is only when the car has turned the corner and gone out of sight that I realise that the excitement has left with James.

'Come on now! Back inside!' says Mama, shooing us three into the house.

I catch Clementina's sleeve as we go in. I feel startled.

'When is he coming back?' I ask, hoping it won't be too long after tea or maybe tomorrow.

'He's not coming back, STUPID, he's gone to BOARDING SCHOOL.'

She tugs her sleeve away from my hand and stomps inside.

How could I not know?

The front door is wooden with glass panes.

The wood is brown and smooth.

There is a shining brass handle at eye-level, if I look in it I see my face a strange shape, a huge nose and my glasses little.

'Now don't dawdle. Upstairs. Nearly tea-time.'

I knew that he was going. I just didn't understand he wasn't coming back.

I touch the brass handle to my face, it is always cold.

Clementina and Kitty are racing up the stairs.

The hall smells of pot-pourri and cloves. The grand-father clock tocks.

'Darling,' says Mama, turning round at the bottom of the stairs, 'darling, do wake up, Doreen will be waiting upstairs.'

I look outside through the window, sort of expecting to see the car still there with James there in it. I look back to the stairs.

I begin to breathe fast. My blood is running cold around my cheeks and all my joints fall loose. Suddenly a kind of panic drops into my legs.

I begin to run. A terrible wind from inside me is holding my body together. I run up the stairs along the landing, run up the next flight, not looking, trying not to feel, run blindly, run through the dark corridor, run round the Egg, round and round the black chasm that drops into the emptiness outside the haunted library, round and round unable to stop, powered by the trembling inside me.

'Tea-time!' says Doreen standing in the doorway of the nursery passage.

Suddenly the feeling closes, I go into a half-dream, I follow Doreen into the nursery and sit where I am told. I notice people's mouths are talking but I can't understand what the words mean. There is a film around things and dots jump about before my eyes. I blink to get them to go away. I look about trying to focus but this strange faraway feeling makes me unable to cross the gap.

After tea, I get down from the table and walk along the nursery corridor in the same daze. I walk around the Egg and into the black corridor. I run through the darkness and then I whisper, 'Don't go away, come back,' but the hollow caverns of the passage only smell musty, and the glass windows reflect the sky.

I walk along the landing to the top of the stairs. The wooden banisters are filled with longing, the staircase is empty, and the hall stretches down to a great cold feeling far far below. I look at the gold birds hiding among the black wrought-iron foliage but they are only made of metal. I sit on the edge of the stairs on the ledge we jump from on Sundays, and I feel along the white shiny paint, I smooth it with my hand. I breathe slowly and whisper 'James' but it makes me start to cry and I am frightened of crying on the cold empty landing and I try to swallow the tears, but I whisper 'James' again, just in case, 'James' until I am crying silently and stroking the long white painted ledge.

Then I have an idea and run down the stairs all the way down past the landing and the letter-weighing scales and into the echoing hall. I climb up the grille on to the flat window ledge to stare out the window. I press my forehead against the glass and look on to the bare circle of grass and the empty road where the car drove away, but there is no shadow left over.

Disappointed, I climb off the sill and open the front door, which is forbidden if I am alone. I wander into the porch. Lying in the corner of the hall window is his balaclava, all squashed up where he threw it this morning. It is for spies to wear when they go on raids and only want their eyes to be seen. I unroll it and put it on. I wonder who to hide from or what to raid. I sniff into the hat and wipe my nose on the wool.

In the garden room Kitty is folding her clothes into her trunk. She is eleven and can pack it up herself. I stand by the open trunk as she folds her blue Aertex shirts, and watch her long careful fingers smooth out the wrinkles. I sidle round the side of the trunk and climb up on the toy box below the window to look into the garden. The wind is blowing the treetops, the sky is grey. The fountain has been switched off and is empty. I wonder about the big toad in the drain.

Kitty comes to sit beside me, and looks out the window.

'D'you want to help me fold my cardigans?'

I look at her, her smooth white cheek, her long nose like Papa's, her green eyes. There is moonlight in her eyes, it shines softly into mine.

I nod slowly, and tears begin to gather in my eyes and

roll down my cheeks. Kitty brushes my hair off my face and smooths it to the side.

'Don't worry,' she whispers, 'he'll be back soon.'

I am crying in full sobs now, and I exclaim through the sobs, 'Clementina said he was *never* coming back.'

'No, not never, a long time maybe, but not never.'

'Will I be seven?' I say, still sobbing.

She thinks a bit and nods, 'Yes, you'll be seven, but that's not long away.'

She gets up and walks to the trunk.

It seems so far away to me that I can't help crying even more.

'Look,' she says, 'you have to fold the dark-blue one along the seam, like this.'

I get down off the toy box, my breath coming in jerks, and help her fold her cardigans.

I stand outside the curved wall at the front of the house, a wall that echoes, and stretches out like a wing and leads to the side door. The other tall echoing wall leads to the gun-room door. I stand next to the little strip of grass, and look at the moss that grows in the cracks. The doves call desolate sounds from the roof. 'Roo-coo, roo-coo, I love you.'

'Come straight back,' Doreen said.

I walk along the grass strip and sit in the shadow outside

the cloakroom window next to the porch, where we play Captain-coming-aboard.

Doreen never even said anything when she found Kitty asleep in my new bed. Maybe she didn't mind. I liked it that Kitty had climbed in with me so I wouldn't have to look down the black corridor. She snuggled right in and we giggled under the covers. And I liked sleeping with her arms round me, my fingers tangling in her curly hair. She has the moon in her eyes, even when the lights are out.

I walk round the edge of the porch, up the step, and stand on the stone with a hole in it, and lean against the windowsill.

'When they've gone, come straight back!' said Doreen.

Kitty didn't cry like she did at breakfast. She just said, 'I'll be back before you're seven because we've got half-term,' but she had red eyes.

I don't want to look in the window. I don't want to enter the echoing house that is so full of emptiness.

I knew that Kitty didn't want to go, she sat in the back and kept swallowing. Clementina sat in the front with Mama and I saw her mouth talking after the car had started moving. She was explaining something with her hands.

I look through the window at the brown shadows, and know that inside it is colder than in the fresh air.

When the car drove away I felt something inside me

being pulled out, it made me want to be sick. It went off with the car but it was still attached to a little thread. The little thread must have got longer and longer as the car drove away because I can still feel it pulling.

I jump down off the stone and my feet echo when they land. I stand very still for the sound to go away. There is the moon in her eyes. I am frightened without her.

I run from port to starboard imagining that Captain is coming aboard. I run up the rigging, and wash the decks. Playing it alone is no fun.

I don't want to go in. The emptiness is too like the emptiness I feel inside. If I go in I will disappear. All the ghosts from the Library and Egg will gather round and swallow me.

'If you want to go downstairs to say goodbye then come straight back up to the nursery when they've gone.'

'Yes.'

I open the hall door. I run across to the front stairs and get close to the wall. I don't want to be near the gold birds because of the monster that has settled down the middle of the staircase. I will be safer if I walk up the edges. I take one step at a time trying not to touch the carpet, holding the little white eggs. I run past the saloon. Ghosts from the library are cramming the air. I run up the edges of the carpet, and my legs begin to wobble. By the time I reach the dark corridor I am breathing fast, I daren't stop. The air is full of empty beings. I run round the Egg and into the nursery.

'Good girl, you came straight back.'

Hugh is on the floor playing with a wooden jigsaw of a clock, Annie is sleeping. I sit down by the nursery fire and tangle my fingers into the grille of the fireguard and watch the flames leap up the chimney.

The huge house echoes with their absence. Corridors are longer and darker, the air seems colder and the garden further away.

I play on the floor of my new bedroom. I am playing with a plastic Indian on an orange horse and two miniature pigs. They live in the wooden apple with a stick of pale-blue chalk.

'Time for bed,' says Doreen, coming in the room, going across to my bed and pulling back the sheets.

I climb in.

'Will you leave the light on?' I ask.

'Yes, the corridor light.'

There is James's empty bed and I am frightened that a ghost will come and sleep in it or just sit there staring at me.

Doreen puts the light out and leaves the door open. I can see along the corridor into the terrible darkness. The white lady might come. I lie awake watching for her.

It is all right, I can hear Doreen and Pauline in the nursery, she won't come if they are talking. But the bedroom door is opposite the Egg and underneath the Egg is the library and they can come up through the hole with their cold breath and clammy inhuman bodies.

I swallow. I watch. I breathe fast. I hear Doreen closing the nursery door. I can't hear them any more, I can't hear their voices. I lie waiting in the cold silence trying not to imagine, trying not to feel or see or breathe, trying not to exist, but the horrifying feeling of something slipping in beside me makes me whisper a low squeal.

'Angel of God!' I whisper. 'Angel of God, my guardian dear.' I can't remember it, I can't remember the prayer. 'Angel of God, my guardian dear . . .' The feelings are in my throat, I daren't breathe them in, bristling slippery monsters, eyes that look at you. 'Angel of God, my guardian dear, ever this night be at my side . . . ever this night be at my side.' I am whispering it out loud, my feet are feeling each other in panicking circles, I want to cry out, to scream, but then they would have me, they would lift me out of my bed. 'Angel of God, BE AT MY SIDE.' I can feel tears on my cheek, my body quivers, the terror is sharp and cold. 'Angel of God.' I begin to sob quietly. 'Angel of God,' I beg.

Suddenly with a clap, it is there, standing in the thundering silence of its outstretched wings. It is lit by gold threads. It flickers. Diamond shapes of black and gold and green are on its dress.

I know it is there for me.

I draw my knees up to my chin and squeeze my eyes shut.

But I do not sleep, and into the trembling of my half-awake dream a voice speaks:

I am the red earth and
the green shoot,
the orange-bellied newt in
the swollen water.
I am the howling night
and the first light,
the blue dusk, and the
twisted root.
I am the lashing rain,
the spotted egg,
the hissing flame.
Look for me in sunlit water shadows and the grass in dew,
seek me in the hearts of flowers and the gentle sound of the doves,
for I am with you.
I am with you along black corridors and by the edge of the black
chasm.
I am with you in the lonely darkness and the longing of the day
and I hold you with the stillness of the hills.

In the half-light of the old nursery I have been sitting, staring at the sky. The room has grown chilly although the wind has died down. Suddenly a bat flies in through the open window and flutters round the room. It swoops out through the crack. I'm glad it doesn't fly against the glass. I get up to close the window and watch the bats playing low-flying acrobatic games across the grass. A large pale moon is rising behind the trees. The sky is turning faded blue and the thrushes and robins are calling chirrups and melodies from the trees. Something in me shivers and breaks open. I look out on to the fields of grass in the moonlight and breathe a sweet air from the garden. I stay watching for a long time as the moon rises and grows smaller and brighter. The light is white and soft. I feel it touching my face. The sky is turning cobalt blue and stars begin to appear above the swaying trees. A moon breeze lifts my hair, it feels warm. The leaves shiver as the breeze passes through them. I think of James and Kitty.

ACKNOWLEDGEMENTS

Barbara Turner-Vesselago, Alexandra Pringle,
Victoria Hobbs, Rosemary Davidson, Richard and
Marigold Farmer, Harold Klug, Kisty Hesketh,
Alexander Hesketh, John McEwen, Anjum Moon,
Louise Page, Mary Sewell, Emma Tennant,
Matthew Yorke, Annie Gillies, Francesca Pugno-Vanoni.

A NOTE ON THE TYPE

The text of this book is set in Linotype Janson. The original types were cut in about 1690 by Nicholas Kis, a Hungarian working in Amsterdam. The face was misnamed after Anton Janson, a Dutchman who worked at the Ehrhardt Foundry in Leipzig, where the original Kis types were kept in the early eighteenth century. Monotype Ehrhardt is based on Janson. The original matrices survived in Germany and were acquired in 1919 by the Stempel Foundry. Herman Zapf used these originals to redesign some of the weights and sizes for Stempel. This Linotype version was designed to follow the original types under the direction of C. H. Griffith.